ONE BRAVE SUMMER

Ann Turner

ONE BRAVE SUMMER

HarperCollins*Publishers*

One Brave Summer
Copyright © 1995 by Ann Turner

Library of Congress Cataloging-in-Publication Data
Turner, Ann Warren.
  One brave summer / Ann Turner.
    p.   cm.
  Summary: Katy spends the summer in the mountains with her mother, an aspiring writer, and learns a great deal about life from her adventurous new friend Lena May.
  ISBN 0-06-023732-5. — ISBN 0-06-023875-5 (lib. bdg.)
  1. Friendship—Fiction. 2. Fear—Fiction. 3. Authorship—Fiction. 4. Mothers and daughters—Fiction. I. Title.
PZ7.T8535On 1995   94-18702
[Fic]—dc20   CIP
                                           AC

Typography by Al Cetta
1 2 3 4 5 6 7 8 9 10

First Edition

To Anna, with love
—A.T.

ONE BRAVE SUMMER

stood under the cottonwood tree in our new yard. I still wasn't used to it; the size of it, how the shadows lay like dark water along the edges of the lawn. I wasn't used to the new house with its too-bright shutters and its neat front steps.

I was waiting for Ma to come home from teaching, and I heard something rustling next door, by the house where that teenager, Penny Roberts, lived. When we first moved here, her hair was blond. But somewhere around Christmas, she dyed it black, with a streak of purple down the side. She reminded me of a bird, a sad bird.

I saw that she was standing in the shadows of her yard close to someone. I heard low murmurs. Then the guy she was with kissed her. I could see that, even in the shadows. A shaft of sunlight showed the streak of purple in her hair, but it didn't show me who she was with. They seemed to be dancing slowly, back and forth. Was Ma home yet? I looked at my watch; 3:30; she'd be home soon. I looked up. They were still kissing. I looked down. Thirty seconds had gone by. I shifted on one foot.

Where was Ma? She knew how I hated being home alone, especially in the new house. I checked my watch. One minute and forty seconds had gone by since they started kissing! They still danced, pressed together. Two minutes had gone by. The blinking lights on my watch reminded me of the heart machine in TV movies that blinks and blips when someone is sick. I checked the time again. Two minutes and seventeen seconds!

Ma's car turned into the driveway. Penny and the guy stopped dancing. There was daylight between them. And as she stepped back, I could see that she was crying.

Chapter 1

"The mountains?" I screeched, not believing what Ma was saying. "Why are we going to the mountains?"

Ma sat across from me, sipping iced tea. "Because it's hot, Katy."

"Well, it's been hot before, but we never went to the mountains. I just don't want . . ." I stopped. It was hard to put into words.

"You don't want what?" she asked softly.

"Too many moves, Ma. First, we had to move to this house . . ." She waved her hand like she was going to say something, but I rushed on. "I know, I know you think it's a better school, but I had to get to know a *whole* new group of people, and now you want to move again!"

She pushed at her hair. It was wild and frizzy, with streaks of gray in the front. "Well, I thought it would be good to get settled in too, Katy, but I just heard about this cottage from a friend and I thought it might be a chance for us." She paused. "A chance," and stopped.

A chance to do what? I picked up my Popsicle and began to suck on it. On the other hand, if we went to the mountains I wouldn't have to worry about keeping up with my new friends—such as they were. There weren't all that many.

"If only we'd stayed in the old neighborhood— the school wasn't *that* bad, Ma," I said, going over that old argument.

"We've talked this all out before," said Ma. "That school was not good, and you were not getting the education you deserve. That's why we moved. The first year's always the hardest, Katy. Next year, fifth grade, will be good. A nice cool summer in the mountains is just what we need. We can settle in together, and it will give me a chance to work on my novel."

Her novel—the mysterious thing that she worked on every evening after she put me to bed. I could hear the keys tapping away in the downstairs living room. Sometimes I thought she cared more about her novel than she did about me.

And so, three days later, with the back of the car piled high with her typewriter and our bags and suitcases, we drove up the long, winding road to the mountains.

"Do you see they're blue?" Ma said, gripping the wheel. She hated driving, and drove like someone in a war movie piloting a plane—eyes straight ahead, hands tight on the wheel.

"Yes," I said. I was surprised. I'd started out feeling angry, carrying in my pocket my mad list of all the things I wasn't going to like about this summer:

1. There will be no one I will like.
2. There will be nothing to do.
3. Ma will write all day, and I will be bored.

But as we drove through the blue, humped shapes of the mountains, all the anger seemed to flow out the window in the clean, cool air. Pines leaned over the road. We went through small villages lined with white and blue houses. Some had gingerbread along their roofs; "cottages," Ma called them.

Then we came to Sugar Cove. There was an old horse fountain filled with red flowers. Two cats sat in front, licking their paws. The gray cat had its pink tongue stuck out, like it had forgotten it. Two kids sat eating ice cream cones on the steps of a general store. The steps sagged like laundry on a line.

Ma said, "We'll come back for groceries and stuff after we settle in. I can't wait to see the cabin. Can you find Hays Road, Katy? It's supposed to be the first right turn after we go through the village."

I looked and sure enough, a fork went off to the right with a green sign saying, HAYS ROAD. "Mr. Hays lived here years ago," I said. "He was famous for his enormous purple tomatoes. And they named the road after him."

"Ha!" Ma chuckled. "I like that, purple tomatoes. Maybe they taste like grapes."

The road went upward. The trees were thick along the side, and the road was like the bottom of a river, full of holes and rocks. I couldn't see any houses, just a few weathered mailboxes beside the road. The sky seemed to get bigger and a brighter blue as we went up.

At the top of the ridge, Ma turned into a shaded lane and drove under the trees. "I think this is it." She turned off the ignition and opened the door.

"Oh," I said, climbing out of the car. "Oh, look!"

The mountains tumbled away into the distance, a soft blue. The wind was sharp and clear, and I could smell pine and cedar. The cabin was a small brown house with a porch set on gray rocks. There was a steep roof pulled down over the porch like a baseball cap against the sun. A big marmalade cat scooted under the front steps and disappeared.

I climbed the steps to get into the shade while Ma went exploring. The shade felt sweet and cool, and the wind blew in my face. "Maybe," I said to myself, "just maybe," thinking that the summer might not be so terrible.

"Maybe what?" came from a dark corner.

I jumped.

"That's a good jump," said the voice, "at least a foot. I was afraid you might be a sorry sort of person, afraid of everything."

"I'm not afraid, and who are you anyway!"

This person got up from a twig chair and came forward. She had the reddest, curliest hair I'd ever seen on anyone, and she wore a white T-shirt wih a pair of electric blue shorts. She had pink jellies on her feet.

"That's good, you can talk. Want a sourball?" She handed me a green striped one. I saw it was the same green as her eyes.

"I'm Lena May." She rolled the ball into the corner of her cheek. "Lena May Martin. You?"

"Katy," I sucked the candy. "Katy Ann Williams."

"Well, Katy Ann." Lena looked at me. "I've been waiting for you all morning. I sure am glad you're here. This is a lonesome hill to live on—mostly old people and only one baby. I love babies, don't you?"

"Not really," I answered. "They smell bad and they cry a lot and they can't talk."

"My, you're fussy. How about old people? You like them? Mrs. Parson's had some great adventures." She paused and eyed me again. "I just love adventures. Do you?"

I sucked and swallowed. "It depends on what you mean by adventures."

"Well, you are a careful sort of person. I mean sky-diving, riding horses too fast, swimming in deep water, scaring people on the road at night."

"Maybe. That's not the kind of adventures we have in the city."

For a moment, she looked almost sad. "What kind of adventures do you have in the city?"

I didn't answer. I keep quiet when I don't have anything to say. It's part of being careful, and I like to be careful. Besides, I couldn't tell her that my life was as dull as those old cats by the fountain. You can't make an adventure out of getting up, getting dressed, going to school, coming home, doing homework, watching TV, and going to bed to the sound of Ma's typewriter tap-tapping away downstairs.

"Maybe," she snorted. "That is a weak and wobbly word."

"Maybe," I repeated.

Then Ma came up the steps to the porch and introduced herself to Lena May, inviting her inside for some iced tea.

Lena May said, "I'd like that, but another time, Mrs. Williams. I've got to get home to my Gran or she'll begin to worry. I promised her that as soon as

I saw the new people, I'd come on home."

"Do you live nearby, Lena May?" asked Ma.

"Oh, just three houses down the road. You can't miss it. We have a mirror ball in the garden and the neatest flowers you ever saw. My gran bullies them into being neat. If they aren't, she rips them out and throws them away!" She hopped on one foot and laughed.

Ma laughed with her, and suddenly I felt left out.

"Well, see ya," Lena May said, and jumped down the steps. She was the jumpingest person I'd ever seen. We watched her run down the lane and turn onto the road until she was out of sight.

"I think you're going to have a good summer, Katy," Ma said, rubbing my back. "I think Lena May's going to be a lot of fun."

"Maybe," I answered, and went inside to the cool of the house.

Chapter 2

Ma carried the battered blue case toward the house. She stopped outside the door and breathed in. Her lips moved.

"Saying a prayer?" I asked.

"Yes. Beginnings are important, Katy. The Navajos know about that; they bless houses when they move in. That's what I'm doing."

I was glad Lena May wasn't there to see Ma standing in the porch gloom, her lips moving fast and silent.

"Why don't you pray for money, Ma?" I couldn't

help saying. "Ask that your new novel will make a lot of money." That was something I could understand. Then we'd have enough so she could send me to one of those camps where you learn to do theater and tap dance; that's where most of the kids I met this year in the new school were going. I wish I could've said I was going to camp instead of a cabin in the mountains.

"No." She turned and smiled at me, holding open the screen door. It was dented in the front, as if some little kid had smashed his hands up against it. "I never wish for money, you know that, Katy. I'm wishing for a strong character for my novel." She strode into the living room and put her typewriter on a side table. "I just know I'll find one up here. These hills and hollows are full of wonderful, strong people, not all flattened out like city folks."

I bristled. "I'm not all flattened out and I live in the city—and so do you!"

"Well, but we're different. I wasn't born in the city, and you—you're just special." She smoothed my hair and rubbed my back. "Just special," she repeated.

She knew I was mad at coming here this summer. I kept my back stiff, not wanting to let her soothe me down. I wasn't going to like this, see if I didn't!

"Oh!" She spun around. "I just love this place. Look at that old twig furniture, real stuff with blue rag pillows. Let's look around." She grinned at me.

Slowly, I followed her into the kitchen. It was a small room with a table in the center, covered with a red checked tablecloth. Open shelves were over the deep sink. "That sink's like Grandma's, Ma."

She ran her hand down the sink's side. "Mmm, these are the best kind—soapstone. And look out the window."

I came and stood beside her, but not too close. A golden meadow ran down a slope to a big oak tree at the edge. Pine and oak were thick along the edges, making dark, cool places on the grass. I saw sunlight shining on water. I wondered for a moment what it would be like to step out of that cool, safe dark into the hot light of the meadow.

I swooped upstairs, wanting to be first, to find if it was as awful as I figured it would be. The stairs were steep and dark. I had to hold on to the wall. The wallpaper came away in little peels under my fingers. There was a hot, atticy smell. "Probably wasps up here, Ma," I shouted down.

I poked my head in the first of two bedrooms. It had a slanty ceiling and yellow rose wallpaper.

"Look at the quilt, Katy." Ma came in and sat on the iron bed. The quilt was made from red and blue rosettes and rustled when Ma touched it. "This is so beautiful. Just think of those women making this, piece after piece, using up all their bits of old clothing."

I wasn't sure I was going to like sleeping under somebody's old bits of clothing. "I want something new," I wanted to tell Ma. But I didn't.

We went into the next bedroom. There was another black iron bedstead in a blue flowered room. The quilt was made of tiny triangles in all the colors of the world.

"Maybe," Ma said, sitting and touching the quilt, "maybe my character is hiding in here. Look—blue calico. A little girl had this dress, with golden curls and a lisp. She became a schoolteacher and went out West."

I touched a brown triangle. "How about this? Nettie Gray's dress, a Confederate widow who held off the troops with a pitchfork and her goat, Buster."

Ma shrieked. "That's it! Why, Katy, I didn't

soothe me down. I wasn't going to like this, see if I didn't!

"Oh!" She spun around. "I just love this place. Look at that old twig furniture, real stuff with blue rag pillows. Let's look around." She grinned at me.

Slowly, I followed her into the kitchen. It was a small room with a table in the center, covered with a red checked tablecloth. Open shelves were over the deep sink. "That sink's like Grandma's, Ma."

She ran her hand down the sink's side. "Mmm, these are the best kind—soapstone. And look out the window."

I came and stood beside her, but not too close. A golden meadow ran down a slope to a big oak tree at the edge. Pine and oak were thick along the edges, making dark, cool places on the grass. I saw sunlight shining on water. I wondered for a moment what it would be like to step out of that cool, safe dark into the hot light of the meadow.

I swooped upstairs, wanting to be first, to find if it was as awful as I figured it would be. The stairs were steep and dark. I had to hold on to the wall. The wallpaper came away in little peels under my fingers. There was a hot, atticy smell. "Probably wasps up here, Ma," I shouted down.

I poked my head in the first of two bedrooms. It had a slanty ceiling and yellow rose wallpaper.

"Look at the quilt, Katy." Ma came in and sat on the iron bed. The quilt was made from red and blue rosettes and rustled when Ma touched it. "This is so beautiful. Just think of those women making this, piece after piece, using up all their bits of old clothing."

I wasn't sure I was going to like sleeping under somebody's old bits of clothing. "I want something new," I wanted to tell Ma. But I didn't.

We went into the next bedroom. There was another black iron bedstead in a blue flowered room. The quilt was made of tiny triangles in all the colors of the world.

"Maybe," Ma said, sitting and touching the quilt, "maybe my character is hiding in here. Look—blue calico. A little girl had this dress, with golden curls and a lisp. She became a schoolteacher and went out West."

I touched a brown triangle. "How about this? Nettie Gray's dress, a Confederate widow who held off the troops with a pitchfork and her goat, Buster."

Ma shrieked. "That's it! Why, Katy, I didn't

know you made up stories, too. I love that."

I ducked my head, embarrassed. She was the one who made up stories, not me. I had no idea where those words came from.

"And this." She pointed to a shiny black triangle. "Mr. Dearborne's mourning coat. He loved nothing better than attending funerals and crying," she said. "He wasn't really sad, of course, he just liked to cry and give people a good send-off." She laughed. "See, endings are important too, Katy."

"You take this room, Ma," I whispered. I did not want to sleep under a piece of cloth that had seen a dead person—or even ten or twenty dead people. Maybe some of their dead breath had gotten sucked into the cloth. Maybe the tears had soaked in too, and anyone who slept under that cloth would dream of tears and funerals. No thank you!

I ran into the next room and touched my quilt. Red and blue. Nice, cozy colors. Patriotic colors. Nothing to do with death and loss. I looked out the window, over the meadow to the trees. Ma came and stood beside me, putting her hand on my shoulder.

"I know this has been a hard year for you, Katy, and I am sorry. Maybe this summer we can kind of heal up together. I'll write something wonderful, and you'll get to know Lena May and have fun. . . ." She moved her hand and smiled.

I shivered. What did that wave of the hand mean? Adventures and brave things? I thought she wanted me to be brave, the way she was when she was a little girl. Didn't she tell me often enough about all the hair-raising adventures she used to get into? I gritted my teeth and clenched my hands; I was not going to have any adventures this summer. I was not going to do anything exciting. Maybe I would read a very long book, one with one hundred and fifty pages. I knew a girl who did that once. Maybe I would press some wildflowers and take them back to science class in the fall. I touched the mad list that was still in my pocket. I'd have to change that last entry, where I worried about being bored. I think being bored would be a very nice thing to be.

Chapter 3

Ma made breakfast and brought it out onto the porch the next morning; white toast with grape jelly, a plate of sliced apples, and big mugs of tea. We sat in the twig chairs and watched the pines swaying in the breeze.

"Anything you especially want to do today, Katy?" Ma sighed and sipped her tea. She went on. "I just feel like sitting here all day, drinking tea, and thinking about my book."

"Why don't you?" I finished my third piece of toast.

"Why don't I, indeed?" murmured Ma. She got notepaper and pen and sat down with a fresh cup of tea. "Who knows what'll come up if I just sit here long enough?" She grinned at me.

I smiled back, not angry this morning. That fresh, cool wind from the mountains and the birds calling made me forget about being angry. A sudden thought popped into my head; maybe it wasn't all Ma's fault that we moved.

I saw Lena May running up our drive. Her legs in the same electric blue shorts pumped up and down. Her pink jellies shone in the sunlight.

"Hey, Katy!" she shouted and waved. "Up early, glad to see that. Can't waste all day lying in bed. We've got things to do, adventures to have!" Panting, she came and sat in a chair beside me.

There was that word again that I hated— adventures.

"Hi, Lena," Ma said from the shade of the porch.

"Hi, Mrs. Williams. You working? Heard you were a writer. I'm very interested in that."

"I'm *thinking* about writing, Lena May; it's not the same thing as doing it."

"Ha! That's true. Thinking isn't the same as doing. My gran would agree with that. I don't think she does much thinking. There's not enough time with all the doing she has to do."

"And what is that?" Ma leaned forward so she could see Lena May better.

"She has a huge garden and cans tomatoes, beans, corn, you name it. She sews most of my clothes at night after the dishes are put away. Her house is so clean you could feed a baby off the floor. Alice Ackles, my cousin who just moved over from Sweetwater, was saying the other day that she could see her *reflection* in Gran's floor."

"Doesn't sound like my floor, does it, Katy?" Ma said, and laughed. "You could never see yourself in my floor, though you might see other things."

"Yeah, like Fingos stuck to the floor, or bits of yarn from that rug you never finished." I giggled.

"Yeah, that rug was too darn fiddly for me." She stood and stretched.

"But isn't your writing fiddly, Ma?" I asked.

"That's different. I like that kind of fussing with characters, how they talk and move and what they think about. Now you girls can sit here and visit— there's iced tea in the fridge if you get thirsty. I have to go find my character." She straightened her

T-shirt and walked down the drive to the road.

Lena May watched her. "I like your ma, Katy. But what does she mean about finding a character?"

I shrugged and spread my hands. "I don't know; it's a mystery to me, Lena May."

"I could tell her about some characters. I should tell her about my Grandma Wilson."

"What about her?" I inched away a little. I could tell Lena needed room for this story; her arms were already moving around, making little windmills in the air.

"Well, she went crazy. Had to take her away to a place somewhere. She always made me cake after school."

"That's not crazy," I said, "that's nice. That's what grandmas are supposed to do."

"Well, wait, just wait 'til I get to the good bits. She had a parakeet called 'Sweetheart' that she tried to teach how to talk. Don't you just hate those birds? Alice has one, too."

She didn't wait for an answer. "All they ever do is poop in their seed dish and spill water all over the floor. Sweetheart not once, not ever said, 'Want a kiss?' Maybe that's what drove Grandma Wilson crazy."

"How did you know she was crazy?" Talking to Lena May was like being on a jouncy raft on a wild river.

"Oh, sometimes she ran backward up the street at night. She asked people for their covers of *Time* magazine to put underneath her bird. Said he needed something interesting to look at when he pooped." Lena May blew a bubble and sucked it back just before it went all over her cheeks.

"That's funny!" I wished Ma were here. She'd like to hear about Lena May's grandma.

Suddenly, I wished I had something special to tell Lena May. I could tell that she was as full of stories as a store shelf is full of toys. I wanted to show her that I had interesting things in my life, too.

"If I tell you the strangest thing I ever saw, will you tell me the strangest thing you ever saw?" I asked. I actually put my hand on Lena's knee and she didn't brush it off.

"Sure." She blew out another bubble and sucked it back just in time. "I like strange things."

"When we moved to our new house, I saw Penny Roberts—this girl next door—outside one day with a guy."

"So? That's nothing strange."

"Well, I haven't told the whole story. I was waiting for Ma and looking at my watch. And this guy who I couldn't see grabbed Penny and kissed her and kissed her."

I paused for breath.

"Go on. I'm waiting for the strange part."

"They were kind of dancing, Lena May, and they were pressed together so tight you couldn't see any light between them. I timed the kiss on my watch. It went on for two minutes and seventeen seconds!"

Lena stood up and waved her arms. "Two minutes and seventeen seconds? Why not one minute and five seconds. Or two minutes and seven seconds. Why seventeen?"

"That's what I ask myself," I said, feeling proud.

"Then what?" She sat down again, staring at me.

"Then, when they stopped kissing, Penny was crying."

"Hmmm, crying. Maybe she was disappointed? It wasn't very good? Maybe he was a lousy kisser. Maybe his teeth hurt her; I'm not quite sure what happens to your teeth. Do you know? Do they stay inside your mouth or not?"

I shrugged. I didn't have any idea what happened to your mouth, your teeth, your lips, or your nose.

Lena May put her hands in her hair and frothed it about for a bit. It reminded me of Ma. "We'll just have to do some research on that, Katy. Maybe Gran will know. She kind of makes a hobby out of love—listening to all the stories of who's going with who, which one's getting divorced—she knows a lot about the mystery of love. Like a dance, you say?"

She jumped down to the grass and swayed back and forth. "Maybe love is like a dance, Katy. And we'll find that out when we're older."

"And have breasts and high heels."

"Yeah!" She howled. "They come together. You go to the store and say, 'Can I have some breasts please—my young cousin Tina calls them *breastes*— and some nice high heels to go with them?'"

I jumped down to the grass beside her and smiled. I'd told her my story and she hadn't laughed at me. I hadn't told anyone about what I saw that day because I was afraid people wouldn't believe me. Then I had to ask, "What was the strangest thing you ever saw?"

We sat down on the steps together and Lena May smoothed her hair back. "Oh, I saw a baby get born once. My cousin Alice was pregnant with her first baby. Gran and I were visiting when suddenly Alice falls onto her rug and tells Gran she's got the most terrible gas pains!"

"Gas pains? Is that what having a baby feels like?" I'd sort of been wondering about this, what it really was like and would it ever happen to me.

"Well, it did to Alice, I guess! She's kind of fat and maybe she couldn't tell what she was feeling. Anyway, Gran told me to call the EMT people and go into the kitchen to make tea and not to come out 'til she said."

"And?" I said. "Did you see anything? What was it like?" This was better than TV.

"Katy, when Gran tells you to go into the kitchen and not come out 'til she says, you *stay* in the kitchen and don't come out 'til she says! But just after Tina was born, she told me I could look, if I wanted."

"And?"

"Babies are awfully little. And she was kind of white at first, but then she cried and turned red. I gave Gran a clean towel and she wrapped the baby in that. Alice was crying."

"Why? Was she sad?"

"No, silly! Because she was so happy. Women always cry when they have babies. And then the EMT people came in the ambulance after it was all over and took Alice and the baby to the hospital. But they were okay."

I was quiet. Lena May really knew a lot more about things than I did. Here I was, trying to figure out an old kiss, and she'd gone straight to the top and almost seen a baby get born.

Then Ma came swinging up the drive, notebook in hand, smiling. I could tell she had some good ideas. They were locked up in that old book like jewels in a chest.

"Having fun, girls?" she said, hopping up the steps past us.

"Yes, Mrs. Williams. We're telling our life histories," Lena said.

"Great!" Ma said in a faraway voice. "That's just great."

Why did her voice have to be so far away? Couldn't she stop and talk to us before she went in to work on her book? I clenched my hands on my knees.

"Now," Lena whispered to me as the screen door banged. "We are going to work on that mystery of love, Katy. I'll talk to Gran tonight. . . ."

I put a hand out. "Don't tell her it was me that saw them kissing."

"Don't worry, I won't. On second thought, maybe we'll just have to look around on our own. Hang out by the road some moonlit night and see if any lovers come walking down the road. Maybe they all kiss for two minutes and seventeen seconds but nobody's ever timed them before!"

I grinned at her. "Maybe so!"

"But I bet they don't all cry when they're done kissing." Lena May jumped down the steps and ran out to the road, waving her hand. She sure did come and go fast.

Chapter 5

"Let's go exploring, Katy," Ma said the next morning. We were sitting on our twig chairs on the porch. The sun was climbing in the sky and I knew it would be hot, the kind of hot where it felt like you wore a wool hat in the middle of August; the kind of hot where sweat rolled down and caught in the hollows behind your knees.

"Go where, Ma?" I munched on my grape-jelly toast and sipped my juice.

"To town, the library, the road, out back,

wherever." She waved her hand vaguely.

I looked at her. Was this supposed to be an adventure? She'd never said so in so many words, but I thought she wanted me to be braver and more adventurous. Wasn't Ma always telling me the wild things she'd done when she was young, to teach me about being brave? Like the time she climbed to the top of the butternut tree and her mother had to call the fire department to come and get her down with the hook and ladder truck. She hadn't been afraid, she was only four years old, and was singing "Rock-a-Bye Baby" when the fireman took her down. Or the time when she went swimming in the stream out back by herself and got swept downstream and only saved herself by holding on to a sunken log. She said it was very exciting and she hadn't been scared at all. I wondered if maybe it was *smart* to be afraid sometimes.

"Maybe," I said. "It depends."

"Didn't Lena May say she didn't like the word 'maybe'?" asked Ma, smiling.

"Yeah, she did," I said shortly. I wanted to say, "Not you, too!" but I didn't. I thought about Lena May being dressed in bright sequined clothes and belting out songs. I thought of me being dressed in brown and working in a bank. Suddenly, I jumped up and said, "I'm ready whenever you are. I'll go get my knapsack."

When we met on the porch fifteen minutes later, Ma was dressed in khaki shorts and hiking boots, with her T-shirt that said "Wherever I go, there I am" on the back. I had on shorts, T-shirt, and my navy blue backpack. I'd put in fluffernutter sandwiches and two cans of lemonade. I was sick of healthy food; I wanted sugar today!

We walked down the hill into town, the sweet, cedar air blowing into our faces. It was hot, but not so bad you couldn't go for a walk. We'd be home before the heat clamped down tight. We went into the library and took out some books. Ma got a huge one about Ireland, and I chose one about Pippi Longstocking that I'd already read before. I liked books that I knew the endings to; there were no surprises. And if I didn't know the ending to a book, I'd flip through and find out if everything turned out all right. Then it felt safe to read the book.

As I put it in my pack I said, "Ma? Did you ever think that Lena May is like Pippi Longstocking?"

Ma tucked her book in her knapsack and

laughed. "Yeah, she is, isn't she, only she doesn't have a pet monkey and a horse."

"No, but she's got red hair and knobby knees. No long black socks, though."

"But she's like Pippi—too big for normal life. I can't imagine Lena May getting dressed for school and going on the bus; it would be too boring for her."

Boring. First I was afraid of being bored; then I thought it was what I wanted. I wasn't sure anymore. Wasn't there something in-between boring and adventurous? Something that was safe but not too safe?

We ran down the steps to the sidewalk and wondered where to go next. We wandered down the walk, looking into the small stores together. Past the general store with the gray steps that sagged in the middle and the dusty window that curved out over the dried grass. I could see old pails and shovels for the beach, hunting mittens, deer lure, and fish hooks in the window.

"How about the cemetery, Katy?" Ma paused by the iron fence outside the graveyard.

I looked in and saw all the headstones marching away over the yellow grass. Would it be scary? I hesitated and finally said, "All right, why not?"

"Let's look for someone who lived in our cottage. The man I rented it from said it used to belong to the Carters for over a hundred years. Maybe those quilts in our bedrooms were made by Mrs. Carter." Ma began to hum to herself as she bent over, looking at the stones.

I saw tall black slabs with angels on them; not the comforting kind but the death's-head kind. There were gray slates with weeping willows on them and words like "Dorothy, Gone Home." I came to four little stones set into the dry grass. Initials were carved on the tops.

"Ma, look. What're these?"

Ma came over and put her hand on my shoulder. "Children, Katy. Look at the big headstone." We knelt by it and traced the words, "Helena Long, aged thirty-five years, beloved wife and mother." Underneath were the four names that matched the initials: Mary, David, Daniel, and Isabel.

"What a pretty name, Isabel," said Ma. "Like the mother wanted to give something beautiful to that poor baby. The baby only lived two weeks."

"What did they die of, Ma?" I was beginning to feel a little queasy.

"Usually diarrhea, honey. People called it 'The Summer Complaint,' but it was fatal for little babies. They couldn't keep enough water inside to stay alive. Did she ever get a baby who lived?" Ma traced her finger down the stone and then looked at the grave beside it.

"Ah, Arthur, son of Helena. Good, he lived to be sixty years old! That's better. Poor Helena."

I stepped back, onto the road. I hated the thought of standing on top of those little bones, those babies who never got to be children. "Ma, let's get out of here. It's too spooky."

She took one look at my face; I *felt* white, and she put her arm around me. "Sure, let's go find a nice place to have our lunch."

We almost ran out of the graveyard, and I didn't take a deep breath until we were outside the fence. I was afraid of breathing in some of that sickness from long ago.

I walked close beside Ma down the street until we got past the houses and came to a long field. A hill sloped downward, and there were rhododendrons growing, making deep shade underneath. We climbed down the hill and sat in the shade, unpacking our lunch.

Ma put out some fruit and granola bars. "I know, I know, just humor me, Katy. I have to have something healthy. I feel sick if I don't." She pursed her lips like someone feeling sick and it made me laugh.

"Me, too." I put out my sandwiches, the white stuff oozing on to the crust just the way I liked it. The lemonade puckered up my lips after the sweet sandwich, and in the cool shade, things seemed all right again. I stopped thinking about those tiny baby bones under my feet and the sad mother, and just thought about eating.

"I'm having a good time this vacation," said Ma, with her mouth full.

"Me, too, Ma." And I meant it. I thought I'd hate it here, but I didn't. And even though Lena May scared me a little, I couldn't wait to see what new thing she'd tell me about.

"If I could only get my character right," sighed Ma. "She just isn't doing what I want her to."

"Can't you *make* her do what you want?" I asked, pulling up weeds by the path.

"No, I can't. I know it seems silly, but characters do things on their own and I have to follow them around, taking notes. This one is sentimental and silly, I don't know why." Ma frowned.

"Why don't you use Lena May in the book, Ma?" I said. "You could kind of grow her up, with breasts and high heels, and see what she would be like. She wouldn't be sentimental!"

"Ha, I guess she wouldn't!" Ma stood up, brushing the crumbs from her shorts and shrugging into her backpack. "But I can't see her in high heels. Cowboy boots are more like Lena May." She paused. "But I can't really use Lena in my book—that would be like an invasion, somehow."

"Yeah, I understand that. Ma? Do you think we could pick some flowers and bring them by Gran's house on our way home? We've been here almost a week and still haven't met Lena May's grandmother, and it seems rude."

"Well, it is, you're right. Let's pick some wildflowers and take them by her house."

We bent over and began to pick the flowers of the field; black-eyed Susans, corn-cockle, crown vetch, yellow mustard, and some cloudy white flower I didn't know the name of. It made me think of long-ago times and suddenly, I thought of all the women who came to this hollow to pick flowers before us and sit in the shade. Maybe I was standing on a piece of ground Mrs. Carter stood on fifty years ago. I stood up and sniffed the breeze. I felt almost shivery thinking about it.

"Ready, Katy?" Ma called from across the field. "Let's go to Gran's." We met by the hill, and as we went up the steep slope, Ma took my hand. Hers felt small but strong, and we swung our hands until it got too hot to keep them together anymore.

When we got to Gran's house—it was just the way Lena described it; a neat ranch with blue shutters and a mirrored globe outside in the flower garden—Gran was outside in the front garden, digging. I didn't see Lena May.

"Hello," Ma called as we came up the drive. "We just had to come introduce ourselves; it seems so rude to be neighbors and not know each other. I'm Rachel Williams, and this is my daughter, Katy."

Gran rose from the dirt, dusted off her blue work dress, and held out her hands—both of them. She seized Ma's hand and patted it again and again.

"Oh, I've heard so much about you from my Lena. You're a writer, aren't you? How Mrs. Carter would've loved to have a writer living in her cottage!"

"Oh, you knew Mrs. Carter?" Ma asked.

"I certainly did, and she loved books and stories. But you all come into the kitchen and have some cool root beer. It's getting too hot to be out in the sun. I was just finishing up my geraniums, telling them I'd give them the business if they got gray mold again this year."

She went before us up the front steps, down a cool hall to the kitchen. It was probably the neatest room I ever saw. There was nothing out of place; not a cloth on the counter, not a speck of dirt on the clean tiled floor, not even a drip of water on the faucet. Gran waved us to the shining table, washed her hands at the sink, and took a brown jar out of the fridge. She poured foamy root beer in two blue glasses and handed them to us.

"Try that," she said softly, and stood by the table.

The drink was cool and sweet and trickled down the back of my throat like some stream from heaven. I'd heard the minister talk once about the streams that made the heart glad. *This* made my heart glad.

"Oh, my," Ma sighed, and sipped again. "Oh, my. Why, I haven't had root beer like this since my daddy died."

"I know, it takes an old-time daddy to make root beer like this. This is from a recipe my husband, David, used to use. 'Course, we use water from our deep well, and that is as sweet and pure as a baby's kiss."

Ma laughed. "I can see where Lena May gets her special way of talking—from you, Mrs. Martin."

"Grace, please, call me Grace," said Gran.

"Where's Lena May?" I asked, wiping my mouth.

"She went into town to see her cousin Alice and her two kids. They just love Lena May. They eat her up like she's a piece of candy," Gran said, and laughed. Finally she sat at the table with us.

"Tell me more about Mrs. Carter, will you please?" Ma asked.

"She was the sweetest lady I ever knew. She never had a bad word about anybody, even when she talked about Mr. Cleaver, the meanest man this town ever saw. He was so mean he made snakes cry. Mrs. Carter always said he could whistle well. She was very proud of her tomatoes, and on her property she had about fifty cats—wild ones, tame ones, half-wild ones."

"I think we have one of hers right now," I said.

"There's a marmalade cat living in the dirt crawl space and she just had babies."

Gran smiled at me. "I know, Lena May told me all about it. She loves watching things get born."

I noticed Grandma Martin didn't tell the story about Alice Ackles's baby being born on the living room rug. Maybe that wasn't a story for strangers. Except now I didn't feel like a stranger, and I don't think Grandma Martin did either. For she took the flowers we gave her, put them in some pink flowered jugs and turned to us.

"I think this is going to be the best summer we've had in a long time. I think we are going to be friends."

Chapter 6

"**H**ow're those baby kittens doing, Katy?" Lena May asked, as she bounded up the steps the next morning. She pushed a sour ball into her left cheek and smiled.

"I guess you'll die with a sour ball in your cheek, Lena, like those cowboys who die with their boots on."

"I will, Katy, I will." She offered me a green candy and said, "Let's go see those baby kittens."

We went around back and crawled in under the kitchen. I still thought about spiders, but at least I went in with Lena. I watched the kittens; some were curled up napping and some were nursing on the momma's belly.

"Nice," said Lena, backing out into the sunlight again. "I like to see babies get bigger and move out on their own. Just like *we're* going to move out on our own, Katy. Time for an adventure, I think."

I noticed she didn't ask it as a question. "Like what?" I asked cautiously.

"Whatever we like. There's the creek in the woods with the deep pool. We could go fishing for crawdaddies and see if the old king snake is still there."

I shook my head. Snakes were on my list of things I didn't like.

Lena counted off the second adventure on her finger. "Then there's Mr. Lawton's store. He's got some nice dead people for sale in there. That'd be fun." She looked sideways at me.

"Dead people! I don't believe you."

"Well, come and see them if you don't believe me." She made as if to set off down the drive, but I grabbed her shoulder. I knew there couldn't be dead people in a store, but whatever it was, it might be scary or creepy.

"What else?" I asked.

"Well"— she counted off on the next finger— "there's my uncle Bob's farm and he has a wonderful pig there, Horatio. He's real smart. We could feed him and see what's happening."

I nodded. "That sounds good." We couldn't get into much trouble with a pig, I thought. Didn't they just lie around and grunt?

I told Ma where we were going and she made us lunch. Lena May watched her.

"Strawberry sandwiches! I never thought of that. I never even knew anyone who thought of that!"

Ma cut six fat strawberries and put them split side down on two pieces of buttered white bread. She sprinkled sugar over them and slapped on the top pieces, wrapping them in wax paper. Then she stuck in two cans of lemonade.

"Thanks!" Lena May grinned. "Wait 'til I tell Gran about this. She's always looking for new recipes. How's the writing going, Mrs. Williams?"

"Oh, okay, I guess," Ma answered, sitting down to some iced tea and her notebook again. The squiggles on the white paper looked like angry, dark snakes.

Lena peered at the notebook and said, "That looks like my songs when I write them. I never get it right the first time, do you?"

I was jealous of her talking with Ma this way, as if they shared something special that I couldn't. I gave Lena a little push toward the door. "Come on, if we're going to have an adventure, let's get going."

Ma called after us, "No! I never get it right the first time either, and not the second, and not the third! I'm working on the sixth time now. See you later, girls."

We set off down the steps, the backpack bouncing against my shoulder blades. "How far is it to your uncle Bob's farm?" I asked as we headed down the hill to town.

"Not far, just the other side of town."

We passed the old horse trough filled with geraniums. The same gray cat with the stuck-out pink tongue was sitting in the sunlight. We walked by Mr. Lawton's store, filled with deer lure and plastic beach pails, and headed past the school and the cemetery. I didn't say anything to Lena about all those little baby bones I'd stood on yesterday. I didn't want to talk about it.

Round the curve I saw a snug white house set on top of a hill with fields spreading out on either side. We trudged up the drive. Sweat trickled under my backpack. We pushed open the door and Lena May hollered, "Hello!" but no one answered. "Must be in the fields," she said.

I followed her down the steps to a wooden pen with a low shed at one end. In the shade lay an enormous, dusty, pink pig. Its little eyes were shut tight and its tail flicked up and down. I wondered if it was a sign of bad temper, that flicking tail. Maybe he'd want to bite me? I stood way back from the pen.

"Hello, Horatio. How are you today?" Lena May picked up a long stick and began to scratch his back.

He snorted and opened one tiny black eye. "Mmmmm, doesn't that feel good? Scratch that back, poke that back, help that pig get on his feet!" she sang. "Come on, Katy, help me scratch this monster."

Slowly, I picked up a stick and touched his side gently. I didn't want Lena to think I was afraid of an old pig.

Horatio heaved himself to his feet and stepped closer to the railing. "Careful!" I stepped back.

Lena May laughed. "He's just a baby, Katy, a great big baby." She rubbed between the pig's ears. He strained to get closer, grunted, and put his front hooves on the boards.

"Ho, this pig likes me! He knows I speak pig talk." She began to grunt and squeal, and pretty soon we were laughing so hard she couldn't make piggy sounds anymore. It didn't matter because Horatio was carrying on all by himself.

"Grunt, snort, grrrmmm," he groaned. The boards creaked, I shouted, and Horatio crashed through.

Lena May jumped to the side. The pig's eyes gleamed and he began to run for the hill, heading down to the road. His little tail whirled behind. He picked up speed, like a runaway pink dump truck.

"Whooh, he's gone! Don't even bother chasing after him." We saw a cloud of dust spurt up, then Horatio disappeared around the bend.

"What will your uncle say?"

"He won't be happy. We'll have to take his truck and some slops to get Horatio back," she said. She waved to a small stocky man coming toward us across the grass.

"Hey, Uncle Bob, Horatio's out. He broke through the fence. It wasn't our fault, honest, he just got all excited 'cause I was talking piggy talk and" —she waved her hand— "and . . . "

"He kind of burst out!" I finished, and we both giggled.

Uncle Bob looked at us sternly. "You can laugh, girls, but you're coming with me in the truck. Fetch some slops, Lena."

We found a pail filled with some wilted greens, old corn bread and mash and followed Uncle Bob into the battered green pickup. "I got some beer too, in case the slops don't work." He held up a can of Budweiser and grinned. "Funny how animals just love beer."

When we finally found that dratted pig, he was in a ditch by the side of the road, snorting and wallowing in some really good mud. Uncle Bob headed for him, holding out the slop pail. "Cush, cush, here piggy, nice piggy." He sloshed the pail so the pig could hear. Horatio lifted his head a second, then poked his nose back into the mud. His tiny black eyes closed.

"Pig Jacuzzi," Uncle Bob snorted. "Here, you son of a gun." He threw away the old slops, poured

Chapter 7

I woke to the sound of rain and something tip-tapping. I couldn't decide if it was water dripping from the roof or the sound of Ma's typewriter. After a while, I guessed it was the typewriter because the tips and taps were far apart. There was a flurry of them, a long silence, then a groan. She was stuck. I was almost glad she was stuck; then maybe she'd have some time for me.

I climbed out of bed and went downstairs.

"Want some tea, Ma?"

Ma sighed, staring at the page as if it might jump up and bite her. Her lip was tucked under her teeth.

"Why do you do it, if it's so hard? It doesn't look like fun."

Ma sighed again. "No, it's not fun; it's not *supposed* to be fun."

"Then why do it? Don't work today and do something with me."

"I can't, Katy, I can't, soon, but not just yet. I have to work this problem through first." She stared at the page in the typewriter.

I noticed she didn't answer my question. I slammed cupboard doors in the kitchen, hoping she'd hear. Then I boiled up water in the kettle anyway and poured it over the tea leaves in the blue and white china pot we always took with us. After toasting a bagel, I spread it with cream cheese, and carried it into the living room.

"Eat, it will help. It always does." I wanted to help her, even though I was mad at that stupid book and all the time it took.

"Nothing always does." She pushed herself away from the table in the living room. That was her study for the time we were here. Her papers were spread all over the table and drifted onto the floor.

"I can't stand it, Katy." She plunked herself down in an easy chair and took the cup of tea. "Thanks, honey. I get an idea, I flesh out a character, I spend days, weeks, *months* thinking about it, and finally it takes off like a jet into space. Whoom!" Her hand shot into the air.

She sipped the tea. "Then something happens. Mind rot sets in. The character grows warts, the idea sickens and dies, and I'm left in the middle of the desert with no water, no food, and no way of getting out."

I tucked myself into a chair nearby and munched on a piece of toast. "You'll get out, you always do. Somebody comes along and gets to be a new person in the book. What about Lena May? I thought you were going to use her. Then the book'll take off again, 'Whoom!'"

"I told you; I don't use people I know in my books. It's not fair to them," said Ma. "Who would choose to be a writer, who?"

"I would" came from the doorway.

We looked up as Lena May danced inside.

"You're lucky you can write." She came and

leaned over the table, reading the page stuck in the typewriter. Even I didn't do that!

"His eyes drew in at the corners and he felt the familiar sinking sensation in his stomach. 'How did we get here?' he asked. 'What went wrong? We used to love each other.'"

"Hey, that's dramatic, that's full of life!" Lena May spread her arms and began to sing, "How did we get here? What went wrong?"

Ma winced. "I think it sounds better as a song. Maybe I should give up writing novels and write songs."

"But Mrs. Williams," Lena May said, sitting on the floor and crossing her legs, "what went wrong and how come he didn't know how they got there? I always know how I get to places."

Ma waved her hand. "They weren't talking anymore. They didn't have anything to say to each other. He never told her he loved her. They never did anything together. Their marriage was a shambles."

Was she talking about her marriage to Daddy, a long time ago? I didn't dare ask.

"A shambles, that's a good word." Lena May rolled it around in her mouth, as if it were a sour ball. "I've seen a lot of marriages like that. First the bills come pouring in. ·Bills can kill a marriage faster 'an anything, my cousin Alice Ackles says. Then he starts to stay out late with his buddies, drinking, and before you know it, they're divorced."

Ma peered at Lena May. "How do you know about all that? You're supposed to be a kid; kids don't know about that."

Lena May smiled. "I watch people, Mrs. Williams, I watch people and I keep my ears open. You wouldn't believe what people say in front of kids. They think we don't understand, but we do." Her hair bobbed as she nodded her head vigorously. "We do."

"Well, why *do* people stop loving each other, then?" I asked. Now was the time to find out. "When you get married, everyone thinks it's going to last forever. Why doesn't it?"

"Bills," said Lena May, popping some gum in her mouth.

"People change, honey," Ma said, finishing her tea. "They want different things. Love changes."

"Yup, it sure does. I remember when my cousin Alice Ackles got married, she wore the prettiest white dress with this little cap on her head, though it looked kind of funny because Alice has a big head and this hat sort of popped up during the ceremony, like those things on turkeys that pop up when the meat is done. She wore a white dress and did all the right things, and still they stopped loving each other."

"I'm not sure that wearing a white dress has anything to do with love, Lena," Ma said.

"Well, maybe not. Anyway, before you knew it Alice had two kids and Billy, her husband, stayed out later and later until Alice told him he could leave. He took up treasure hunting, you know with those little metal things you swing over the earth. He was always away hunting treasure."

"Maybe he wanted money because he didn't have love anymore," Ma said.

"I just think people change. Look at Katy and me. This summer we're good friends, having adventures and all. But next summer you might come back and like tap dancing and baton twirling and we wouldn't have anything to say to each other. Not your fault, not mine. That happened to me before with another friend."

"Not me," I said. "I'm never changing."

We ran up the steps to Mr. Lawton's store and hung out beside the magazine racks. There were magazines with women with huge lips, looking like they might eat you up. There were biker magazines, gardening magazines, and just about anything a person might be interested in. Some lady started talking next to us, to a friend of hers. They both had kind of bluish hair, very solid-looking shoes, and puffy ankles.

"So I told him to forget about getting the paper; it took him so long to get ready, Ethel!"

"Slow, that's what he is, slow. Isn't that just like a man to dawdle his time away? Why couldn't he just *get* you the paper, like you asked?"

The ladies shook their heads and I looked at Lena. We wouldn't learn anything about love here. We went through the door and walked across the street to the post office. A group of people were hanging about inside, looking at their mail.

"Junk mail, junk mail," said an old man with hair in his ears. "I'm sick of junk mail. Don't people write letters anymore?"

Nobody answered him. A young guy with a baseball cap on backward sidled up to a girl with long blond hair. "Tonight?" he whispered.

Clutching her pile of mail, she nodded and went out the door. "Darn!" said Lena in my ear. "The only likely candidates just left on us. I wonder where they're meeting? By the gravel bank? Out by the river? Maybe we could go see."

I shook my head. I did *not* want to be wandering around in the dark spying on people.

Outside the post office, we sat on the cement steps and looked at each other. "Maybe love isn't something you can listen in on, Katy. Maybe you have to *do* it, or be in it, like wading in a river."

"Maybe," I said, not knowing the answer. All I knew was this: If I could learn more about love, then I might understand why Ma and Daddy stopped loving each other so long ago when I was only three.

one want to go to a funeral?"

Ma came in front of me and looked at me; her eyes were green and soft today. She was paying attention today. "I don't know. Maybe it's part of seeing life, Katy."

"How can seeing a dead person be part of life?" I grumbled.

"Well, it's the other part of it, isn't it, Katy?" Ma smiled, took my arm, and led me back out to a twig chair on the porch. Sitting me down, she handed me a plate of toast spread with grape jelly. It looked so pretty and cheerful, those little purple-colored toasts in the bright sunshine; not at all like the beginning of a day when I would see a dead person.

"You don't have to go, you know," Ma said, finishing her tea. "Or I could come with you, if you like. Come to think of it, I'd kind of like to see a funeral myself."

I thought for a moment, watching a crow wing out across the grass to the tall pines by the edge of the road. Crows weren't afraid; crows dove in the air and chased away big hawks. Death didn't frighten *them*. But I didn't want Ma there; she'd probably take out her notebook and start scribbling in the middle of the service. And I didn't want Lena to think I needed my mother to come with me.

"Thanks, Ma, but I think I'll go by myself. Lena May's seen all this stuff I've never seen. Ma?" I paused and nibbled some toast. "What if it's scary? What if the box falls onto the ground or, or . . ." I couldn't tell her everything I was afraid of.

"If you get scared, then just come right home. Don't wait for Lena May, and don't stay there if you don't want to. Are you sure you wouldn't like me to come?" Ma refilled my cup with tea, put in milk and one spoon of sugar.

"No thanks, Ma, this is something I need to do by myself. I don't want Lena May to think I'm . . . "

"Afraid?" suggested Ma.

"Yeah, that." We finished our breakfast in silence.

An hour later I was ready in my one good dress, waiting on the steps when Lena May arrived. This time she didn't bounce down the driveway; she glided like someone entering a play from the wings. Like a ghost in a play.

Wearing a blue party dress, Lena May slid over the dirt drive. I don't know if it was the right kind of clothes for a funeral, but she looked pretty. Her

"Now, now," I could hear her murmuring. "Bear up, Violet, bear up!"

But Violet didn't bear up. Just next to her on the grass were two large black dogs. A man in a shabby black jacket held them tightly on leashes.

When the minister got to the words, "Ashes to ashes, dust to dust," Violet swayed against one of the dogs. He lifted his nose and howled, a long, mournful note. The dog next to him lifted his nose and began to howl too, the notes drowning out the minister.

The minister tugged angrily on his robe and glared at the dogs. The man in the shabby black coat jerked on the leashes, but this only seemed to excite the dogs more. Howling louder, they rose on all four legs. Violet tottered toward them, weeping, and picked up a clod of dirt to throw into the open hole. She stayed on the edge for a moment, teetering back and forth, tears streaming down her cheeks.

"Watch out!" Lena called. Somebody yelled, "Step back, Violet! Step back, honey!"

As Violet teetered on the edge, one of the dogs grabbed her dress and jerked her away from the hole. She collapsed on the ground and the dog licked the tears from her face. The howling stopped, and we could hear the words of the minister again, "I am the resurrection and the life."

I didn't know if I was going to laugh or cry; all I knew was, I was seeing real life, not something in a movie or a book. Looking around at the other people by the grave, I saw tears were rolling down their cheeks. But their faces were bright and flushed. They watched Violet as the large woman helped her to her feet and looked at the dogs, now quiet. They were seeing life too, and they liked it. The ropes squeaked as four big men let the casket down into the ground.

The minister finished. Some people came forward and threw dirt onto the casket. The thudding sound made me shiver. I kept thinking of the woman inside, her little gray face, and the dirt falling on top of the casket. Was she afraid, too?

"I'm going up, Katy, want to come?" Lena May asked.

"No, no!" I stayed, even though my feet wanted to pick me up and run right out of there, right back up the hill to where Ma sat drinking tea on our cool porch. But I didn't move while Lena May went up to the grave, grabbed some dirt, and threw it in. I watched her come back, bouncing over the grass.

She was too excited to glide. I shook my head and unclenched my fists. *Stop being so afraid, Katy!* I told myself. *Nothing bad is going to happen. The body's in the ground, and it's almost over. Relax.*

One of the dogs gave a last howl, Violet blew her nose, and people began to come up and press her hand, telling her that her sister had gone to a "better place," and "it was God's mercy that she'd been taken."

Did God "take" people when they died? Did He come and snatch you away from life to go do something else? Like feeding angels? Or combing the sheep in God's pastures? They never tell you about the really important things.

Turning from the grave, people kissed each other, shook hands with the minister, and got back into their cars.

"They're going to Violet's house for some really good food," whispered Lena May. "Hickory-cured ham, baked sweet potatoes, coleslaw, and that thing with pineapple rings and little marshmallows, whatever you call it. Mmmmm. It's important to eat after you've buried someone, don't you think?"

I nodded and we walked back to the drive. "I guess so."

"Weren't those dogs the best part, Katy?"

"It wasn't a *play*, Lena!" I walked faster, still shivering a bit.

She kept up with me. "Sure it was, Katy, sure it was. You tell your ma about Violet's dogs and how Violet almost fell into the hole. She'll like it, I bet. She won't get all fussy, like you."

"I'm not fussy, just respectful, Lena May. We're supposed to be quiet in a cemetery, aren't we?"

We walked through the gates onto the sidewalk, heading home. The air was hotter now. I stopped shivering and rubbed my arms.

"I guess," Lena May answered, "but I'd rather have dogs at my funeral and someone almost falling in the grave. That's drama, that is! Nobody'll forget this funeral for a long time!"

I began to laugh. "No, they won't. What if she'd fallen into the hole?" I had a sudden picture of Violet's head disappearing into the earth as the dogs howled.

"Why, they'd get her out, of course, throw her a line, like you do when someone goes overboard." Lena May giggled and had to stop, she was laughing so hard.

I leaned against her, laughing until I cried. It

wasn't until we started up the hill that I remembered something important; this time I saw a different part of the movie—the end and not the middle. I was scared, but I didn't run away. That was the kind of person I thought Ma wanted me to be. I was proud of myself for the first time in a long while.

Chapter 9

"**H**ow was the funeral?" Ma asked when Lena May and I wandered into the house.

"Pretty good!" I answered. "For my first funeral, I mean."

"What did you expect?" said Lena May, plunking herself down in a cool corner. "A band?"

"Well, I didn't expect dogs!" I said. Then I smiled. They really had been something, those dogs, howling away while leaning against the man

Lena May snorted. "There it is again, that word—'maybe.'"

"That's a weak and wobbly word," we all said together.

"Would you girls like some lunch?" Ma said. "We can sit in the shade on the porch and eat it."

We went into the kitchen with Ma, and Lena May sliced up fresh tomatoes while I buttered the bread. Ma poured out milk and put crunchy ginger-snaps on a plate. We all helped take it out to the porch.

"I don't understand how your character can run away on you if you talk about her too much. It sounds like magic, Mrs. Williams, like you need spells or something to make it work." Lena May sat down and took up a sandwich.

"I could use a spell or two right about now," sighed Ma.

"Maybe we could help," said Lena May. "I know a lot about love from watching people in town and listening to Gran. And I've seen someone get born." She took another enormous bite and chewed rapidly, while Ma swiveled around to stare at her.

"Seen someone get born, Lena May? When, where?"

Lena May swallowed quickly. "I saw my cousin Alice Ackles have her first baby on the living room rug."

I nudged her, hard. I knew she didn't see *everything*.

"The rug? Why wasn't she in the hospital?" asked Ma, sounding confused.

"She got took real fast—thought she was having gas pains, I guess! Anyway, I didn't see the whole thing, just the best part when the baby was in Gran's hands and cried her first cry."

"Mmmmm," Ma said dreamily. "I remember when Katy was born. She just slipped out like a little seal, but she didn't cry. She looked around the room with these wise, old eyes. They're still wise, old eyes." She reached over to pat my knee.

I smiled, pleased. I hadn't heard that story in a while; I liked the part about being "wise." Maybe Lena May wasn't the only person around here who knew something.

"You girls have any plans for this afternoon? Maybe you need some quiet time after that funeral. Want to grab some books and read in the shade of the porch?"

Lena May looked at me and shook her head.

"Later, Mrs. Williams. Now Katy and I have to do some research. Thanks for the lunch!"

I nudged her again. I didn't want to talk about our research in front of Ma yet. What if she laughed, or thought I shouldn't have seen Penny Roberts kissing that guy? Maybe she'd ask me a whole lot of questions I couldn't answer. So I jumped up, took our dishes into the kitchen, and headed for the door. Lena May followed.

"Remember those two in the post office the other day?" Lena May asked as she skipped down the drive. "I wonder if she cried after he kissed her."

"I don't think so," I said, running to keep up with her. "They looked like they knew a lot about kissing."

"It's like this, right?" hollered Lena May. She seized a thin birch tree. "You grab 'em tight. And you plant your lips like this." She smacked hers up against the bark. "Then you sort of grind 'em around while you make mmmmm-ing sounds, like this." When she stopped, her lips were covered with white paper bark, and she wasn't smiling. "That didn't feel very good. It's got to be a lot better than *that* for you to catch me kissing somebody!"

"Maybe that's why Penny Roberts cried," I said, starting to skip down the road.

"Why?" Lena May ran to catch up with me while she brushed at her lips.

"Because kissing him wasn't any better than smooching that old birch tree!" I laughed and ran ahead.

Lena May hooted and followed me. "Do you think it ever *is* better than kissing a birch tree?"

I stopped in the dirt road, puzzled. "Well, it's got to be better. Isn't that how we get all these babies? Doesn't it start with kissing? Why don't you go ask Alice Ackles about it?"

"Yeah, maybe I will. I'm a little confused about the details—what comes between the kissing and the babies."

I felt good, running along beside Lena May. I was going to find out something this summer. I was going to get some answers to some of the questions I'd had rattling around inside of me like coins inside a jar.

Chapter 10

The next day when Lena May came I was ready for her. Maybe I was changing, because I was looking forward to an expedition. I'd already packed a lunch and stuck it in my knapsack. After saying good-bye to Ma, we set off down the road. We didn't talk very much at first, just a word here, a word there, like birds in the trees.

Ma says the birds are noisy at the beginning of the spring when they are mating and building their nests. That's when they wake me up in the bedroom back home; they're singing and hollering in the branches. But by July, they've sort of settled down. They nag a little at each other in the morning, Ma says. She tells me that the birds aren't really saying beautiful things to each other, even though the sounds are beautiful. They're saying things like, "It's *your* turn to get the morning worm. Isn't! Is! Isn't! Is! I got it yesterday. Well, I got caterpillars yesterday, so there! And while you're up, take out the trash!" That's what Ma says the birds are saying.

I told Lena May all that and she hooted so loud a grouse jumped out of the bushes, scaring us. I skittered off to the side, and I was glad to see Lena May's face got sweaty when the bird burst out at us.

"I think that's what a heart attack must be like!" Lena May said when we'd calmed down a little. "Just a huge bang of sound like that." She whammed her hands together and another bird took off into the blue. I guess Lena May's the kind of person who scares birds.

"You know where we ought'a go?" she asked me, walking kind of close to my side.

"Where?" I was sticking pretty close to her, too. It's just on days like these, when the wind blows lure; and some sweaty-looking mittens.

"Lots of good stuff in here, yes, sir!" Lena May marched up the steps and pushed the door open. "'Lo, Mr. Lawton, how are you?" she asked.

A very large man stood behind the candy counter. He had suspenders holding up his pants, except it looked like they were attached to his tummy and held that up, too. Little puffs of gray hair lay like dust on his head, and his face shone in the heat.

"Hello, Lena May," he said kindly. "And what do you want today? Jujubes? Chocolate-covered raisins? Though in this heat the chocolate will all come off in your hands. How about some nice red licorice?"

I don't know about other people, but I despise licorice. And I especially despise red licorice. It isn't even the right color!

"No, no thanks, Mr. Lawton." She pointed to some gray balls in a box. "How about some of that mummy candy? Don't they look like mummy eyeballs, Katy? Oh, this is my friend, Katy Williams. Katy, this is Mr. Lawton."

We nodded at each other, and I stared at that candy. There were little white spots in the middle with gray all around. My stomach gurgled.

Mr. Lawton chuckled. "Always joking, Lena May, always joking. Nope, I'm out of mummy eyeballs. Those are mummy fingers." He smiled and tipped himself forward on his feet.

"I'll have some mummy fingers, then." Lena grinned at him and held out a quarter. He put a bunch of stuff into a paper bag and handed it over.

"And I'd like one of those cherry lollipops, please," I said, putting a quarter down on the counter.

"Mind if we look around your store, Mr. Lawton?" asked Lena May.

"Nope, go right ahead." He went back to his chair in front of a fan and took up his paper. It rustled in the breeze.

I cleared my throat. I still felt a little wobbly inside. Lena May patted my arm.

"Just a joke, Katy Ann, don't let it upset you. It's just antique candy, is all." She took out a dusty stick and offered it to me. I shook my head. "Come on!" She darted around some shelves piled with chocolate chip muffins and Frito chips.

I looked and looked but couldn't see any Barbie dolls. I think if they had been there, their dresses would've been in tatters. And maybe they'd have white hair. I guess Lena May was bored too, because she said, "Let's go back to my house and have root beer with Gran."

She ran out the door and I followed, down the street heading toward the hill out of town. Trees shaded the road, and we ran in and out of patches of sunlight. The sun was hot on my head for a few seconds, and then cool again, like someone was taking a hot cap on and off my hair. We walked up the hill, turned left at the top, went a bit further, and stopped in front of the little white house with blue shutters.

I stopped by the mirrored ball on the lawn and looked in it. A huge face with a balloon nose stared back at me. I stepped back. "Whooh! I look like an alien, Lena May."

She came and peered over my shoulder. Her red hair disappeared in one side of the ball, and it looked like flames along the other side. We looked like two evil sisters.

"I don't like that thing!" Lena May turned and ran around the back of the house. "Come on, Katy!"

Gran knelt in the dirt, weeding the geraniums.

She was talking to them as she worked.

"Now grow right, this time. Red blooms, please, not any of those feeble old pink ones. And no gray mold this time, please, God."

"All set, Grandma? You tell them how to grow?" Lena May said.

Gran looked up and smiled. Suddenly, the lines went sideways and I was looking at a beautiful lady, someone hiding inside her skin and wrinkles.

"Katy, here you are!" She took my hand between both of hers and shook it gently. Her hands were warm and dusty from the earth.

"Come inside, come inside, you two. You've been getting all sweated up running along the road, I can tell." We followed her inside.

Gran bustled to the refrigerator and took out a dripping mason jar. She wiped it with a blue cloth and set two glasses on the table. "Here." She poured out the foamy drink.

I tasted it, letting it roll back down my throat. It was as sweet and sharp as last time, with a coolness that tasted of deep well water. I put my glass down.

"It's still wonderful, Gran." I knew it came from a recipe of her dead husband, and wished I could ask what happened to him. But I didn't dare ask.

Lena had never talked about him. Did everybody in her life just disappear?

"My ma is still talking about this root beer, Gran. She wants the recipe, though she says it probably won't taste the same in the city 'cause the water's different," I said.

"She's right, Katy, it won't taste the same. You'll have to come back every summer so you can visit us and have our root beer."

She patted my shoulder, and we went outside again. It made me feel sad to think about going home in a few weeks. But Gran said we'd have to come back. I watched her looking at her garden like a commander inspecting troops. She pointed to some flower I didn't know and said, "That one's got deep roots. It's got to be watered real good for it to grow right. Like me." She smiled. "I've got deep roots and I'm never leaving Sugar Cove. But my Lena here, she's like a plant with shallow roots. You could move her and she wouldn't die." She ruffled Lena's hair, and I wondered if that's why it was so fuzzy, from Gran loving it up so much.

Suddenly, Lena burst out, "That's right, Gran, that's right. Someday I'm going to move away from Sugar Cove and write beautiful songs that make people cry, all about love and death and babies. I'll be famous and wear a sequined jacket and build you a house so big you could drive a car into the kitchen!" She stopped and flushed, the red seeping up her cheeks.

Gran patted her hair again. "That's my girl. I don't know about the drive-in kitchen and the sequins, but I like the part about songs that make people cry."

Love and death and babies. Gran didn't even act surprised. I guess she knew Lena May's secret heart and loved her anyway. I wanted Ma to know my secret heart too—that I was afraid of walking over baby bones in the earth, that I didn't like sleeping under pieces of black cloth in quilts, and that I could never be adventurous the way she'd been when she was little.

Chapter 11

When Lena May said good-bye to me that afternoon, she whispered in my ear, "Don't be surprised if something happens tonight. It's time for us to do some more research on that mystery of love."

I asked her what she meant, but she only winked mysteriously and patted me on the shoulder. I went home feeling like a cat with its fur fuzzed the wrong way. I wanted Ma to pat my hair the way Gran did Lena's, and I wanted Ma to know my secret heart the way Gran did Lena May's.

But when I opened the door, Ma was busy tap-tapping away on the typewriter and only murmured that she'd be done "in a bit." How would she ever get to know my secret heart if she didn't pay any attention?

"In a bit!" I said that night, climbing into bed. "Ha! That bit was a whole afternoon!"

Ma came and stood in the doorway of my room. I turned my head away.

"Katy? I'm sorry I didn't spend much time with you today, but I just *had* to keep writing. If I stopped, I would've lost it." I didn't look at her.

She sat on the edge of my bed and patted my shoulder. "Tomorrow, I promise. We'll spend tomorrow together. We can take a hike to the creek out back or go swimming together."

I murmured something that sounded like a word but wasn't. Ma patted me again and sighed. "I'm trying, Katy, I really am. We'll have a nice day tomorrow." And she got up and left my room.

I tussled with my pillow, trying to find a comfortable spot. It was as ornery as I felt. Finally, I went to sleep and dreamed of trying to ride a huge blue horse across a rushing stream. I woke up to the sound of something hitting my window. I sat up and listened. There it was again.

I went to the window and looked out.

"Yo, Katy!" a small figure called softly. It had to be Lena May. I called back, "Yo!"

"Come on out! It's time for an adventure." I could see her grinning; the moonlight shone on her white teeth. The last thing I wanted to do was go on an adventure. The shadows moved across the lawn and her face. Everything looked mysterious and scary.

"What kind of adventure?" I finally called back.

"You don't ask what *kind* of an adventure, silly! Just come on down and we'll figure it out together!"

"What kind?" I asked again.

"Not scary," she said. "Just for fun."

But was her idea of fun my idea of fun? Maybe she thought doing scary things was fun.

"What kind of fun?" I called down.

She waved her arm at me. "Come on! Don't be so scared!"

I didn't call back this time. I wasn't scared, just careful. But I didn't want her to think I was a coward, so I pulled off my nightgown, dressed, and went downstairs. Ma would never hear. She slept like the dead. Out the front door, and there was

Lena May with a knapsack on her back and flashlight in hand.

"What's the flashlight for?" I kept my distance from her.

"In case we need it on the dark road. It's time for us to find out more about romance, Katy Williams, why Penny and that guy kissed for so long and why she cried at the end. We'll never find out unless we try to listen and see some other people kissing."

"I don't think I want to do that." I planted my feet in the grass. "Isn't that spying? Couldn't we get into trouble for that?"

"Pooh!" She waved her hand. "Weren't you spying that day you watched Penny and the guy next door?"

"I didn't *mean* to be there; it's different."

Not answering, she grabbed my hand and pulled me down the drive. She had to work real hard there for a time because my feet just didn't want to go on that dark and shadowy grass. The moonlight made strange shadows on the ground—fringed, ragged things that looked like flying bats, but turned out to be leaves blowing in the wind; long, sharp shapes that darted and stabbed at the dark. I shied sideways, wondering what they were, until I saw that the pines made those shadows. The air smelled sweet and thick with patches of coldness that we kept running into. Something called from the woods; a creaking, shrill sound. I stopped dead and my stomach churned.

The sound went on and on, "*Waaaah, creeeaaak, waaaaah!*" Then it went, "*Woppit, woppit, waaaaah!*" I was so afraid I couldn't even move. I was so scared I thought I would pee in my shorts.

Lena May waved a hand in front of my face. "Hey, Katy, wake up! It's only a screech owl calling. Come on!" She led the way onto the road.

Wiping my face, I took a deep breath, not sure I could go ahead with this. I turned and looked back at the house. Ma always kept a lamp burning on the table in the front room. I could see the warm glow of the light from the end of our drive. It called to me; it said, "Safety, warmth, coziness." I stood on one leg. But if I ran back now, Lena May would call me a coward. Ahead, I saw her stop quickly and dart into the bushes. Following, I came up to her side and crouched under a big pine. It shushed in the wind and sent its sweet smell over us.

"Shhhh." Lena May waved her hand down. "Someone's coming."

We waited. The screech owl kept on calling, breaking through the dark with its hard, strange sound. It made my skin ripple up. Did having adventures mean always being afraid? But Lena didn't seem scared.

I heard a footstep on the road. Then another. There was the faint sound of someone humming off key. Lena May waved her hand again, meaning, I guessed, that we should keep quiet and just listen. Then I saw her shoulders stiffen. Her head snapped up and her breath sucked in. I could hardly make myself look out, to see what it was that had frightened her. But I had to. I had to be brave; I had to be something else besides careful.

Crawling forward, I peered through the pine branches. Someone was humming to herself and walking on the road. I could see it was a "herself," as she had on a white nightgown. A person mourning her lost love? Maybe it was the ghost of Lena May's mother!

I rubbed my arms. They were covered with goose bumps. I looked again. The "someone" came into a bright patch of moonlight. Humming, she walked with her head bent. It was Gran.

Lena started forward when Gran got to the edge of our drive. I pulled her back. "No! Let's follow her." I didn't know what was wrong—if she was awake or asleep.

Gran stopped for a moment and raised her head. Her eyes were open. She stared right at us, right through us. Lena gave her a terrible smile and moved her hand, but gran didn't see. Then some words tumbled out of her lips.

"And I said to her don't, I said, just don't. . . ."

I shivered and my teeth chattered as Gran headed back down the road, toward her house.

Lena May sobbed, and I held her tight. "If there's something wrong with my gran, Katy, I just can't stand it. Everybody else went away." She sobbed again and rubbed her nose on my sleeve. I let her, patting her back.

"Come on now," I said softly. "Come on, Gran's going to be okay. I think she's sleepwalking, Lena May."

Lena May kept giving little sobs and hiccups as we walked. When we got to her house, Gran turned into the drive, stopped by the geraniums, and gave them a little pat. She opened the front door, wiped her bare feet on the mat, stepped inside, and went straight to bed. Smiling slightly, she even pulled the covers up to her chin. I think that smile scared me more than anything else she did that night.

"Come on." I led Lena May into her bedroom and found her nightgown in the drawer. I looked at her. She shivered and clutched her arms around her body.

"Do you want some help?"

"No!" She unclutched her arms, undressed, and pulled the nightgown over her hair. She patted her head absently, once, twice, and climbed into bed. "Do you think she'll be okay?"

"Sure, Gran will sleep the rest of the night." I hoped I was right. "You just go to sleep and we'll talk in the morning. Everything's going to be all right," I said, turning out the light.

"Don't do that!" She sat straight up in bed. "I want the light *on*!"

"Okay, okay," I said, switching the light on. I remembered once I had a fever and felt so sick I kept the light burning all night long. Maybe Lena felt that way.

Then she whispered to me, "Thanks, Katy, thanks for following Gran home with me. Are you sure she'll be all right?" Her voice wavered.

"I'm not sure of anything, Lena, but I know your Gran's a strong woman, and I bet my ma can help us. She'll know what to do."

I remembered Ma telling me once about someone who was sleepwalking. When they came back home, they settled down. I didn't think I could stand it if Gran started roaming around anymore that night. And neither could Lena.

"'Bye, call me tomorrow, okay?" Lena asked.

"Sure," I said, and walked out. Locking the front door, I ran all the way home, never stopping until I got through our door and stood in the safe, warm pool of light from our lamp. I climbed the stairs and got under the covers. The quilt at the foot of my bed rustled. I hoped the bright colors would keep my dreams happy and calm. I didn't want to dream about Gran wandering around at night, looking for something—or someone.

But just before I fell asleep, a thought came into my head: You just had an adventure, Katy Ann Williams, and you weren't afraid—you were brave. I pulled the covers over my ears and snuggled into the warm dark.

Chapter 12

I crept downstairs when the sun was just poking over the hill. I didn't feel hungry; my stomach clenched in and my back felt all stiff and achy. Last night I'd been brave, telling Lena that everything was going to be all right. Now, in the morning, I wasn't so sure. What if Gran was falling apart? What would Lena May do?

I walked softly to the phone and dialed her number. I had to know if she was okay and if Gran was okay. The phone only rang once before some-one picked it up.

"Hello?" It was Gran.

"Hi, Gran, it's Katy. I'm just calling, just calling . . ." I couldn't think of a good reason fast enough. My mind felt slow as a bear in a winter cave.

"You're up early, Katy."

"Yes'm, I am. I need to talk to Lena. Is she awake?"

I heard Gran's footsteps going away and then coming back again. "Yes, she is—sitting bolt up-right in bed like she's seen a ghost." Gran chuckled, but I thought she sounded worried.

Lena picked up the phone. "'Lo, Katy." Her voice was thin and tired.

"Everything okay?" I whispered.

"Yes," Lena answered, "I guess so." I knew she couldn't talk with Gran being right there.

"Why don't you come over here for breakfast, Lena May?" I asked. I could hear Ma's quick, light steps on the stairs. The match scraped as she lit the gas stove to make tea.

"Okay, that's a good idea. Like a picnic, Katy." I could tell she was trying to be cheerful because

Gran was there, but her words sounded like stones dropped in a well.

Hanging up the phone, I went into the kitchen. Ma peered at me.

"You're up early. What's going on? Couldn't sleep? Owls bothering you last night?"

How did she know about the owls and that they scared me? I shrugged my shoulders and made a show of getting cereal from the pantry, fetching bowls and setting out the spoons.

"Lena's coming here for breakfast, Ma. She's got . . ." I paused, not sure how much to tell Ma. I hadn't asked Lena if I could tell Ma. "She's kind of got some worries on her mind and wants company," I finished.

"Oh, that's too bad." Ma poured hot water over the tea leaves in the blue and white china pot. "What is she worried about, Katy?" Sitting, she took a spoonful of cereal.

"I'm not sure—maybe Gran. She thinks Gran is working too hard."

"Well, she probably is. Just to have a house that neat means she works too hard, Katy! I don't think that Gran puts her feet up very often."

"No, she doesn't." I sat and had some cereal,

then leaped up when I heard the screen door slam. Lena May came inside and sat at the table. She looked terrible. Her eyes had purple circles under them and her hair looked limp and flat.

"Lena, honey, what's wrong?" Ma said.

"I can't tell you. Yet," Lena May said as Ma gave her a cup of tea with milk and sugar in it.

Ma put her hand over Lena's and patted it. "That's right, just take your time, honey. When you're ready, we're here."

After breakfast Lena and I sat on the steps outside.

"I don't know what to do, Katy," Lena said, rubbing her finger on the stone step. "If anything happens to Gran, I'll just die. She's all I've got—well, except for Alice."

"And Uncle Bob."

"And Horatio," she said, smiling a little.

"I don't think that sleepwalking is a disease, Lena. She's not sick or anything. I've got to talk with Ma about it," I said. "Is it okay to talk to her?"

"Maybe," Lena said, still rubbing her finger against the stone. "Maybe. I don't know what's right or what to do. I always thought, Katy," she looked up at the pines and wiped her nose, "I always thought that if I was good and did my home-work and didn't get into trouble that Gran would live a long time. You know, like making a bargain with God. I'll be good and you'll take care of me. But I don't think it works that way anymore."

I was silent, not sure what to say.

"Things go wrong even if you're good," Lena said, and a tear dripped off her nose.

I put my hand on her arm and squeezed it. I still didn't know what to say, but I wanted her to feel better and stop crying.

Suddenly, Lena jumped up, wiped her eyes on her sleeve, and said, "I think I'll go see my cousin Alice in town. I think I need some hugs from Tina. That'll make me feel better."

"You could ask Alice about sleepwalking, Lena," I said, standing beside her.

"Yeah, I could. Maybe I will, maybe I won't." And she went off down the driveway without look-ing back. This time she didn't jump; this time she didn't run. She didn't look at all like the Lena May I knew.

Chapter 13

"**M**om?" I asked at lunch that day. My eyes were tired and my body felt as if someone had thumped me on the back last night.

"Mmmm." Ma looked like a wind had just picked her up and set her down again. Her hair whizzed off to the side, and her eyebrows were mussed as if she'd just woken up.

"Mom? Do you know anything about sleep-walking?" I fiddled with my sandwich. It didn't look very appetizing.

"Not much." Ma sat down beside me at the table and looked out the window. "It's a beautiful day, Katy. Look at it." She waved her hand. "Why do you ask?"

The sky was clear and blue; butterflies puffed up from tall pink flowers in the meadow. It all looked so normal.

I didn't answer her question. "Do people walk in their sleep because they're sad, Ma?"

"Sometimes. I think they sleepwalk also because they're troubled or worried," Ma said. "Sometimes we don't know why people do it—it just happens."

There it was again—an answer that wasn't an answer. Too many maybes, just like Lena May said.

"Well, don't you *know*? Couldn't you tell when you saw someone sleepwalking if they're worried or not?" I said, putting my hands flat on the table.

Ma shook her head. "Why all the questions, Katy? Did you see someone sleepwalking? Is Lena May wandering around the roads at night?" She stopped and pursed her lips until they looked like one big wrinkle.

"I worry about her, honey, not having any parents. Gran is a wonderful woman and I know

Lena loves her, but to have your one parent be so old! She must be at least sixty-five. What will happen when she dies? What if she dies before Lena is grown up? That's what I'd worry about if I were Lena May's grandmother."

I sucked in a breath. "That's not a worry; that's a mountain to carry around!"

Ma laughed. "That's my girl, that's just what it is. 'Course, it isn't funny at all. And goodness knows how she supports that family." She took a bite of her sandwich. "She's probably got some Social Security—I think you get that when a child's parents die. That must be it." She tapped her fork against her plate. "So who was sleepwalking?"

This was grown-up territory: Social Security, support, money, the future. It made the back of my neck itch. I could see now why Gran sleepwalked, but I didn't answer Ma's question about who was sleepwalking. Lena hadn't told me if it was okay to let Ma know.

I wonder if Ma thought that I was worrying too much. She waited for a minute to see if I was going to answer her question and then she put her hands over mine, looking straight into my eyes.

"Katy? I haven't been spending enough time

with you this summer, have I? I've been so wrapped up in that darn book that I don't know if I'm coming or going. And I promised I'd be with you today. Shall we go to the creek out back?"

I grinned, suddenly happy. To go on an expedition together, just Ma and me! "You bet! I'll be ready in a minute."

We both dressed in khaki shorts, T-shirts, and sneakers. I packed a snack while Ma scrounged up the knapsack and put it on. I stuck in two cans of lemonade and two fluffernutter sandwiches. Ma put in two apples and some carrots.

Outside the house I watched Ma wade through the meadow, holding her arms up so the bees wouldn't bother her. That was just like her, to jump in and never hesitate.

"Field swimming," she called back over her shoulder, laughing. "I'm going grass swimming!"

I hesitated for a moment, but I didn't want her to turn around and see me standing on the edge of the meadow, looking scared. But she did—she turned and waved at me.

"Not many bees, Katy, it's okay." It made me happy that she'd looked back to see if I was all right. So I waded in after her, following her path.

Bees and butterflies spun up out of the meadow as we passed. I almost closed my eyes, thinking if I was going to get stung, I didn't want to *see* it happen. Then, suddenly, we were out, passing through the cool shade of the pines at the bottom of the meadow, on under the cool oaks of the woods. The air was quiet and hushed there. Only a few birds called. As we walked, a sweet, sharp smell rose from the ground.

"Now we're forest swimming," Ma said as I walked behind her on a path that looped through the woods.

We heard the creek before we saw it, a rustling sound like a lady walking in a silk dress. It got louder as we came out from under the trees. Black water spun and danced over the rocks, leaping down and foaming up. It reminded me of Lena May, except she'd lost some of her bounce. I wanted it back, but how?

"Let's sit here." Ma slid off her knapsack and sat on the mossy bank. Taking her sandals off, she looked at me. "Want to go in?"

I looked at the water. Any spiders along the edges? Any snakes? "In a minute, Ma, in a minute."

Ma sat there, dabbling her toes in the rushing

water. I liked it that she waited for me this time, instead of rushing ahead. Maybe she was learning that I was a bit slower than she, that I just needed more time.

"It's not that I'm afraid, Ma," I said softly, "at least not all of the time. I'm just slower than you."

Ma nodded, but did not look at me. I felt her hand rubbing the small of my back. "I know, Katy, I know that. And it's okay to be scared sometimes. My problem was I was never scared at the right times."

"What do you mean?" I took off my sandals, inched closer to the water, and stuck my bare toes in. It was cold!

"Well" —Ma ticked off on her left hand— "there was the time I went horseback riding at my friend Lynn's house, and I didn't wear a helmet though she told me to. I fell off that day and almost hit my head on a rock. Lucky for me, I wasn't really hurt." She looked at me, and ticked off on the second finger. "Then there was the time I went walking on the railroad tracks and the train came. I hopped off under a little bridge just in time."

"Did your ma ever find out about it?"

"Nope, never told her. Only told you. So you

see, sometimes it's stupid to be brave. Sometimes I was foolish and got into trouble." Ma rubbed my back again.

I felt some of the stiffness between my shoulder blades easing out. Maybe it was better to be careful, and all this time I'd been thinking she wanted me to be brave and reckless like her.

Suddenly, she hopped in the water and began to sing "Sweet Betsy From Pike." I climbed in after her and joined in— "who crossed the wide prairies with her lover, Ike." We waded around in the water, singing at the top of our lungs, with the sunlight spinning down through the leaves.

I flicked some water at Ma and surprised her. It dripped from her nose, down her chin. She sneezed and tossed some water at me. It rolled down my face. Pretty soon, we were splashing each other, and our clothes got soaked. We began to laugh and hoot. I could feel things soaring up into that blue sky each time we laughed—like being mad at Ma for moving. And being mad at her for spending so much time on her book. Some of the fears I had went high up into the blue, and I felt lighter and happier.

"Ma," I asked, when we climbed out and stood

dripping on the bank, "remember when I asked you this morning about sleepwalking?"

"Mmmmm." Ma shook her hair like a dog, and water sprayed in a circle.

"I wasn't asking about Lena, Ma, I was asking about Gran." I sat down on the moss and hugged my wet knees. Suddenly, I just had to tell her, whether Lena said it was all right or not.

"Gran's sleepwalking?" Ma said. "How do you know?"

"We followed her last night. Lena May asked me to go on an adventure."

"An adventure at night, two girls all alone? That doesn't sound like an adventure, Katy, that sounds downright dangerous!" Ma glared at me.

"Oh, Ma, we were being careful. We weren't doing anything bad. We only went to the end of our drive. And then Gran came walking . . . walking down the road. Oooh!" Shivering, I rubbed my arms. I didn't ever want to see that again—that smile on her blank face or hear those words tumbling out of her lips!

"It was scary, huh?" Ma touched my arm.

"Yeah, it was. We followed Gran all the way back to her house. I made sure she was in bed and that Lena was in bed, too. I locked the door and came home all by myself," I said proudly.

"Good girl," Ma said. "I don't like you girls being out at night, but that was a brave thing to do, taking care of Gran and Lena."

Brave me. Ma said it; it must be so. She loved brave people.

"But what about Gran, Ma? We don't know what to do."

Ma tilted her head back so the sun shone on her face. "I'm glad you told me, Katy. I think Gran's got a lot on her shoulders. I'm going to talk with her about this, but I'll have to be careful how I tell her. I think she is a proud woman."

"She is. Thanks, Ma." The sky seemed clearer now that I'd told Ma. I didn't have to fix this problem all by myself. Maybe there was a place that helped people who sleepwalked.

Then we opened our pack, took out our fluffernutter sandwiches, and had our snack. The lemonade tasted sour and sharp after all the sugar. Smiling at me, Ma puckered her lips, and I thought this must be the best picnic I ever had. Brave, she called me brave.

Chapter 14

Lena didn't come over all the next day, and when I called, Gran said Lena was out doing errands. I was worried about her.

After I got in bed, and after Ma had come upstairs, I heard Lena calling outside my window.

"Katy? You awake?"

I went to the window and looked down. She looked small and far away. In the moonlight I could see her cloud of curly red hair, though it looked kind of silvery now. I couldn't really see her eyes or mouth, just dark places on her face.

"Yes?" I said.

"Want to go on an adventure?" But the words weren't bouncy the way they usually were with Lena May. The words were slow and sad.

"I don't know about an adventure, Lena, but if you want some company, I'll be right down." I wasn't going to sit there discussing plans with her. She needed me.

She touched my arm when I came down. "Thanks" was all she said. We didn't talk about what we were going to do; I knew. This time I'd brought a flashlight and turned it on the lane leading to the road. We walked slowly, heading for the big pines.

"We don't need to hide, Lena," I said softly. "She won't see us, if she's walking tonight."

"Don't use that word 'walking'!" she said. "It sounds like she's dead!"

I shivered and swung the beam across the grass. A toad hopped out of the light into the safe darkness. An owl hooted in the woods far away, a soft hoot this night. Not like the other night when it sounded like the dark was breaking.

We sat down at the edge of the driveway. Hugging her knees tight, Lena shivered. I could hear her teeth chattering. I didn't feel very cheerful myself, and folded my arms around my body. We sat and stared, and sat and stared. The moon shone down. A tomcat with his tail sticking up walked by.

"Mrs. Parson's cat," Lena whispered. "He's got more kittens hereabouts than any other cat. Probably the daddy of your kittens."

He looked fearless, with his broad face and swaggering body. I wished I could be like him—brave and unafraid.

I could feel fear around us, like dark water we had fallen into. It kept Lena's teeth chattering; it kept my arms tight around my body. It made my eyes feel like they had prickers behind them. My hair hurt where it went into my head. My throat was dry and scratchy. I wasn't sure if I was going to cry or sneeze or throw up—maybe all three. Our fear even had a smell, like somebody's underarms or the way a tarred road smells on a hot, wet day.

Suddenly, Lena stood up. "I can't stand this. It's more than a body can bear, waiting around like

this! Let's walk up the road. Maybe we'll meet her."
She pulled on my arm and did not let go, her fingers digging into my skin. At least she was *doing* something about it instead of just sitting still, I thought.

I walked beside her down the road in the moonlight. We'd walk into the light and shine like ghosts. Then we'd disappear into the dark like some animal going down its hole. I thought if anyone saw us *they* might be afraid.

We walked all the way to Gran's house, but didn't see her. The flowers stood up like soldiers outside her front door. The curtains hung stiff and silent at the windows. Creeping around to Gran's bedroom, we peeked in, on tiptoe. I could see the humped shape of Gran under the covers, moonlight shining on her gray hair.

Lena whispered, "I never noticed how gray her hair is. It's almost white now." She didn't say the word "old" but I knew that's what she was thinking. Her lips pursed and her eyes turned down at the corners, as if she was going to cry. The moonlight showed me that.

We moved away from Gran's window back to

the front door. I didn't know what to say to her. Maybe a grown-up would've known what to say; something like "Yes, your grandma's old but she's not really *old*, Lena. She's got lots of good years left." I didn't know that, so I couldn't say that. I just can't lie to save my soul. I saw that Gran might die any old day, and then where would Lena May be?

Together we went into her bedroom and I saw Lena into bed. Crawling under her covers, she pressed her nose into the pillow. I stood there fidgeting my fingers, wanting to say something to make her feel better. Suddenly, I leaned over and whispered, "I think you're very brave."

"You do?" The words rose up from the pillow.

"Yes. You saw something really scary but you didn't run away. You stayed and went back to protect your gran, to make sure she was okay. That's brave."

She turned her head, looked up at me, and smiled.

"And you helped too, Katy. I'm glad you were with me—and Gran."

"Me, too," I whispered and patted her arm, just the way Ma used to after I'd fallen down. "See you tomorrow," I said, and closed the door behind me, racing down the road as fast as I could to the warm pool of light made by our lamp in the window. I got into bed and let the darkness pull me to sleep.

Chapter 15

I remember Ma telling me what she felt like after I was born. She said, "I was so tired the bones in my chest ached. But, oh, was I happy!"

Even though I wore her out, it was worth it. I felt a little like that; Lena and I had this adventure, it turned into something terrible, but I survived it—even though I was afraid of owls, darkness, and dying. I helped Lena May.

When Lena came and sat on my doorstep the next day, dressed in quiet brown clothes without her pink jellies, I wanted to shout at her: "Put on your old bright clothes. Be sassy and funny. Don't lie down and curl up!" But you can't say that to someone who's seen her only parent sleepwalking and talking to herself.

We stayed for a while, watching the kittens tumble over each other in the sunlight. The black-and-orange kitten raced over to the gray one and jumped on its neck, growling. They rolled over and under each other. Then the black one jumped on those two and growled, so they sounded like furry motors. It made me sad to think I wouldn't see them grow up, that I wouldn't even get to see which homes they went to before I had to go back to my house.

"You'll find good homes for them, Lena May?" I asked.

She tugged at some grass and nodded, not even answering.

I scratched my nose and thought: I had to find something that would put the sass back into Lena May. But what?

"Lena?" I asked. "Would you take me to see your cousin Alice Ackles?"

Lena scuffed her shoe in the grass. "I guess so."

I sighed. This wasn't like her at all, this lack-adaisical stuff. "I sure would like to meet someone who had a baby on her living room rug. What did she do with the rug afterward?"

"They burned it!" Lena said, laughing for the first time that morning. "They took it out into the backyard and had a great big bonfire the day after Tina was born. Everyone drank beer and told stories and had a great time!"

"Wow! They sure do know how to have parties up here." I didn't have a very clear idea of what parties were like, except I knew they were noisy and people did things at them that they didn't usually do.

"Come on!" Lena bounced off the steps and led me down the road. You could tell she wanted to be her old self, racing along. Then I think she remembered she was sad, because Lena slowed down and trailed her feet in the dust. I had to walk slowly so I wouldn't get too far ahead.

We went down the hill together, the wind hot in our faces and smelling of cedar and warm earth. We came to the center of town, past Mr. Lawton's store with the ancient toys in the window and the candy so old it looked like mummy's bones. It still made my stomach squeeze in. We walked by the cemetery where we saw Mrs. Solomon's sister get buried and Mrs. Solomon almost fell in the grave. When I thought about it, I'd seen an awful lot in the last weeks—a quilt with mourning pieces, kittens getting born, a runaway pig, a funeral, and Gran sleepwalking. The whole summer was an adventure!

"Alice lives right up here." Lena turned down a side street and pointed to a narrow blue house squeezed in between two other houses. A rag rug hung over the porch and some pink and purple flowers grew in baskets. A little girl with blond ponytails shouted to us.

"Lena! Hey, Lena May! Come on in! Mom's in the kitchen baking chocolate chip cookies!"

We climbed the steps and went inside. It was pleasant and cool, with doors and windows already closed against the heat of the day. In the corner of the living room was a cage with a blue bird inside.

"Matches the paint outside," Lena whispered. "And he's never said 'want a kiss?' in his whole life!"

I laughed and looked at the rug. This one with blue and yellow flowers was the new one, safe to walk on. But still—in this room a baby was born. You'd think that dratted bird would talk just because of seeing that amazing thing happen. But no, he was dumb, like all the other birds I've seen in cages.

"Sometimes," Lena whispered, "Alice puts little diapers on that bird—she calls him Timothy—and lets him fly around the house."

"No! Not diapers!" I sat down on the nearest chair and howled.

"Are they disposable?" I asked after a while, "or do you have to wash them?"

Lena just grinned and didn't answer, as her cousin opened the door with a plate of steaming cookies. She was a wide, comfortable-looking woman with brown hair and surprising blue eyes.

"Lena May! How nice of you to come visit. Tina was just asking about you."

"Mmmm-hmmmm." The little girl nodded, and her ponytails bounced. I took one of the warm cookies Alice gave me and tried to imagine Tina wiggling out onto the rug of this room. Did she howl when she came out? Whimper? Or say, "Howdy do?" Suddenly I thought, maybe I can ask Alice about that kiss I saw; why it went on for so long. Maybe someone who had a baby on her living room rug would know the answer to that question.

"Lena always had a special feeling about Tina here," said Alice, sitting heavily on the yellow sofa. "On account of being here when she was born." She laughed. "I guess I'll never live that story down!"

Lena chuckled. "I guess you won't, Alice. Gas pains!"

"Well, you wait until you're pregnant the first time, Lena May, and see if you know so much!" Alice said. "You get so fat it's hard to tell where you are and where the baby begins. And there's all sorts of funny aches and pains inside. You can't always tell what they mean!"

I didn't look at Lena and she didn't look at me. But I could see how it made sense. Sometimes I got mixed up myself when I felt things in my stomach; I could be hungry and it felt like I was sick.

"These are delicious cookies, Mrs. Ackles," I said. "Just delicious." She'd made them with those huge chunks of chocolate that didn't quite melt when they cooked.

"Alice," she said, smiling. "Please call me Alice."

I was just thinking about how I might introduce the topic of kissing, when Lena May said, "Alice? Could we see your bird fly around? Timothy?"

"Sure," said her cousin. When she opened the door to the cage, the bird hopped out onto her hand and waited. Alice lifted her arm up, like one of those pictures of an old-fashioned knight letting a falcon fly off from his arm.

"I don't see any diaper!" I whispered to Lena May. She just rolled her sour ball into her left cheek and grinned.

"Whee!" Tina shouted as Timothy flew about the room. He swooped past Lena, whizzed over to Tina and perched on her shoulder for a minute. He brushed his head against her cheek and then took off, up to the top of the curtain rods by the front window. I think he knew better than to come to me. I decided I'd ask Alice about that kiss on another visit. This didn't feel like the right time.

Tina climbed up into Lena's lap and snuggled there while the bird perched and twittered. I saw how people got so crazy about their kids. The way her head fit right under Lena May's chin. The way her hands held onto Lena's arms, nice and close. The way her legs swung back and forth, she was so happy to be there in Lena's lap. And all Lena had to do was sit there and hold her, like the little girl was just breathing her in.

After a time Lena looked over at me. "Time to go, Katy." She handed Tina to her mother who gave Lena a big kiss. Maybe Lena wasn't as lonely as I thought she was. She had more family than I had. Maybe if Gran did die before Lena grew up, Lena could come live with her cousin.

I thanked Alice for the cookies and we set off up the road again. This time, Lena ran ahead and I had to scoot to keep up with her.

Chapter 16

"**G**ran wants you all to come for supper tonight," Lena May said over the phone the next day. "I've been telling her about your Ma's book and how it's all about the mystery of love."

"You didn't ask her about, about . . . ?" I fumbled.

"About Penny Roberts and her boyfriend? Nope, but you can ask her tonight. If there's anybody who knows the answer to that, it's my gran!"

I was silent; I wasn't sure I'd have the courage to

ask Gran. Then I'd have to explain to Ma about watching that kiss, and she'd have things to say about that!

"Is everything okay?" I finally asked.

"With Gran?" Lena answered. "She's out now, so don't worry about her hearing us. She slept all last night. I watched." I heard her sigh into the phone, like wind in the pines.

"I told Ma," I said into the phone.

"Well, maybe she can help. Someone's got to help us, Katy. See you tonight, around six o'clock." The line clicked dead.

I wandered into the kitchen where Ma was scribbling notes onto a pad and sipping tea. Fiercely, she stared at what she'd written, ripped off the page, and threw it into the wastebasket.

"Pooh! Now I've lost it. I thought I had it, but those characters of mine are running amok again."

"What's running amok?"

"Not doing what I want them to do, racing around and doing their own thing." Ma sighed and pushed back her teacup.

"Ma? Lena May and Gran want us to come for supper tonight. I told her we'd come. You will, won't you?"

"Of course, honey, I'd love to. And don't worry; I'll find a way to talk to Gran about the sleepwalking. Not tonight, but soon."

That night we dressed carefully—not fancy, just clean clothes, and Ma brushed her hair really hard so it lay in long curls on top of her shoulders.

I stood back and looked at it. "Nope, it's not you." I mussed and ruffled the ends up so they stood out again. "There, that's better."

When we got to Lena May's, they were waiting for us on the front steps. Gran wore a blue striped dress and white sneakers. Lena May had on her electric blue shorts with a yellow shirt and pink jellies. I could see her all the way from the end of the drive, like a light shining out over the sea on a dark night.

"Well, here you are," Gran said, coming down the steps and holding out her hands. She seized Ma's hands and shook them and then kissed the top of my head. I patted it when she wasn't looking, almost as if I could make it sink into my skin and stay there.

"We've got scalloped potatoes and roast chicken with gravy and dumplings and collard greens and Jell-O with little marshmallows," Lena May chanted as we went inside. The table was all set, with a vase of Gran's flowers in the middle. At each place Lena poured a foaming glass of homemade root beer.

Gran bent her head and said a quick grace, thanking God for friends and food and long summer days. I especially liked the part about the friends and long summer days. I had a sudden catch in my throat, knowing there weren't that many days left.

"It's as good as last time, Grace!" Ma said, sipping the root beer.

Gran nodded and smiled. "My husband, David, used to say that love passes and children grow up but root beer is forever."

"Oh, isn't that true!" Ma smiled and looked around. I knew she was searching for her notebook to write that all down. I was glad there wasn't a typewriter handy.

"How is your book going, Rachel?" Gran said as she handed around plates heaped with food.

"Well, I'm not making as much progress as I'd like. I'd hoped to finish it this summer before school starts. Lena's helped me a lot these last weeks. Every time I get stuck, Lena May gives me an idea—or a word. Once she even sang us a song."

Gran's head turned sharply. "A song?"

"Why, yes, Grace, didn't you know Lena can sing and write wonderful songs?"

Lena's face tightened and she stared at her plate. I was afraid that Ma had just made a terrible mistake. Then Gran began to rub the edge of her glass and smile.

"I remember how much her granddaddy loved to sing. He used to hold Lena May on his lap and sing all the old songs. That must be where she gets it from." She reached out and tousled Lena May's hair.

Lena looked up and smiled. It was all right. Gran wasn't mad. Lena was doing something that came through the family and that made it all right.

Gran went on, "Lena tells me your book is about love."

"Mmmm," Ma said, dabbing at her mouth. "It is about love—people who fall out of love."

"There's a lot of that going around." Gran sighed.

"Gran?" I suddenly asked. "How do people fall in love, and why do they fall out of love?"

Gran took a breath. "It's a mystery, Katy. Some people say it's all in how you smell, like animals liking the scent of one another."

"That's not it!" Ma said quickly.

"Of course it isn't," replied Gran.

"Well, how did you fall in love?" Lena asked Ma. I leaned forward.

"I don't really know, Lena," Ma said slowly. "I think I fell in love with him at our college library. He was always so quiet and studious that I believed he was full of interesting thoughts."

"And he wasn't?" Lena said after a pause, while Ma pushed at her greens. Gran shook her head at Lena, but Ma didn't see.

Ma laughed, a short sound. "I found out he wasn't really full of interesting thoughts; he was just quiet. At first I liked that because my own father was so noisy. But that's not enough to make a marriage last. We just didn't have enough to say to each other, and what love we had didn't last. Talking is what keeps a marriage together, girls, remember that!"

"And loving," Gran said softly.

So they were bored; that was it! There wasn't enough to keep her interested. I could understand that now. Maybe when she tried to explain it to me years ago, I wasn't old enough to understand.

"What about my folks, Gran?" Lena asked. "Tell me again. You'll love this story, Katy." She nudged me.

"Your mother met your dad at a dance—they both loved dancing. He swung her round and round and when the music stopped, they were in love. That's what she said."

Lena hummed a tune to herself. I could see her holding that story close, like something magic. Love coming swiftly out of the sky; love, circling like a dance.

Then I remembered Penny and her boyfriend holding each other as if they were moving to music that day in the shadows. "Gran, do you know why someone would kiss another person for two minutes and seventeen seconds?" I blurted out. "Is that what you do when you fall in love?"

Ma gave me a sharp look. "When did you see someone kissing for that long, Katy? On TV?"

"No, not TV," said Lena, jiggling her foot. "People don't kiss that long on television. It's too expensive."

"Where, then, Katy?" Gran asked this time,

her eyes shining. I wondered if she was laughing at me.

"In my driveway at home," I mumbled, looking at my plate. "I saw the girl next door kissing a guy for that long. I know because I was waiting for Ma to come back, so I was looking at my watch. And then she cried when the kiss was over." I raised my head, waiting.

"Two minutes and seventeen seconds! Maybe they'd never kissed before and thought that was the way you did it. And then she cried!" Gran said, sitting up higher. "That's interesting! Maybe he wasn't a very good kisser?"

Ma nodded. "Or she thought love would be wonderful and it turned out to be slippery lips and somebody who stepped on her foot!"

Gran choked and Lena May began to giggle. Soon we were all laughing, imagining that guy stepping on Penny's foot, and that was the reason she cried.

"Or maybe she cried 'cause she was so glad to get some air!" Lena finally said, wiping her eyes.

"Can't you breathe when you kiss?" I asked.

"Sure you can breathe, through your nose," Gran said. I tried to imagine Gran kissing; I couldn't. I think Lena couldn't either because she gave Gran such an odd look.

Suddenly, I saw it all clearly, the way you see something through one of those telescopes set up by the ocean. You look through the lenses and it's all dark—nothing. Then your dad puts the quarter in and you can see light and bits of land through the lenses. What I saw was this: Love is a mystery to grown-ups, too. They don't know the answers much more than we do. That should have made me sad but it didn't; I felt warmth seeping down my shoulders. I'd asked my question and we'd all talked about it. Nobody had laughed, and now I knew why my parents got divorced. Love died, just the way it once grew—sudden and surprising.

Chapter 17

I never did find out what Ma said to Gran about her sleepwalking. She just set off the next day with a bouquet of wildflowers she'd picked from the field. Lena had come over to visit, and we sat on the steps watching the crows circle and caw overhead.

After a while Lena said, "I wonder what she's going to say to Gran. Gran's awfully proud, Katy. She won't want anyone to know she's got a weakness in her. Maybe she'll pretend she meant to be walking at night." She stuck a sour ball in her left cheek and stared out over the hills.

"No," I said, taking the red sour ball she offered me. "I think maybe Gran will be happy to know. Anybody who can make flowers grow like that without gray mold and keep her house so clean will be able to deal with this. Don't you think?"

Lena rubbed the hair above her ear. It flew off to the side—like Ma's. I suddenly thought how much like Ma she was, with her wild hair, being outspoken and funny and wearing any old thing she pleased. I was more like Gran—careful, quiet, a bit slow. I liked things neat and ordered, or I did before this summer. Now I wasn't so sure.

Lena jumped up. "Let's do something, Katy, let's go somewhere! I can't stand to just sit around waiting to find out what your ma says to my gran. I hate waiting!"

"Me, too." I stood and we went down the road, Lena walking so fast she almost looked mad. "Where are we going?"

"Don't know. I'll think of something. Maybe we'll see someone kissing on the road, who knows?"

"In the daytime?" I ran to catch up.

"Sure, don't people kiss in the daytime? They do on TV."

"I guess so. Ma doesn't allow me to watch the soaps, so I've never seen." I followed her down a side road that ran along a stand of oak and pine. The air was thick and warm, and I took deep breaths of the sweet pine smell.

"I know," Lena said after a while. "Let's go see the piano stream!" She hurried ahead, feet kicking up dust.

"What's the piano stream?"

"You'll see." The sun gleamed in her hair and it shone red, like a coil of copper wire. It looked like electricity could just shoot through her hair and light up some bulbs with no trouble at all.

We walked and ran, walked and ran, down the other side of the hill away from town. After a time, when my shirt began to stick to my back and my shorts felt raw on my legs, she turned off the road, plunged through some bushes, and I followed. I kept as close as I could, afraid of snakes.

I heard water rushing—smelled its coolness in the air. Suddenly we were through the hot bushes and into a cool place where the water hurried and bounced over large gray rocks. A bird perched on a stone and dove into the water, coming up out of the white foam with something in its beak. It hopped onto the bank and ate it, its head bobbing quickly to one side.

Lena went over to a boulder, climbed on top and sat down. She motioned to me to follow. Shade and sunlight moved over us; soft, dark patches from the leaves and blinding white from the sun. Dragonflies flew in and out of the sunlight, their wings suddenly shimmering, then gray in the shade.

"This is the piano stream," Lena said. Her words flowed with the water sounds.

"Why is it called that?" I watched the bird dive into the water again and come up with another bug in its beak.

"My uncle Bob told me about it a few years ago. There was a new bride back across the hill in the hollow who wanted a piano more than anything. Guess she imagined herself plinkety-plunking away in her beautiful new living room, astonishing her friends."

I chuckled.

"Anyway, she pestered her husband and pestered him until finally they had enough money saved to buy a piano. Had it sent down to the depot and unloaded for him to pick up in the horse and cart. She stayed at home, waiting for her gift."

"He collected the present—they helped him load it in back and tie it down—and set off home again. You know how bumpy these roads are, how they slip down real fast and speed uphill. Bad enough in a car, but with a wagon?"

I could just see that wagon bumping along the dirt road, the man looking over his shoulder to make sure the piano was still there.

"They came to the top of the hill there," she gestured, "and the cart began to pick up speed. The horses went as slow as they could, and the man, Homer was his name, pulled on the brake. At first it seemed to do some good, slowing them down around the first curve. But the hill got steeper, there was another curve, and before you knew it, those horses were galloping downhill with the wagon bouncing behind them, swinging wide around the corners. Whoo!"

Lena slapped her hand on her knee. "They hit that last curve right there at about twenty miles an hour, and that piano just flew off over the side. *Bam!* It tumbled down the hill and fell to pieces in this very stream!"

"Wow! The whole thing? Broken into bits?"

"Broken into bits, all the little keys floating downstream like somebody's teeth." Lena rubbed her hands and grinned. "What do you imagine that lady said when Homer got home with no instrument?"

"Don't know. What did she say?"

"Homer never did tell. I guess she said some hard words, and he brought her here to see the destruction. They said she climbed up on this rock and cried for two days before she decided she was wasting her time and she'd learn to play the zither."

"Ha! The zither!" I jumped down from the rock. "Do you think there might be some piano keys in the stream, Lena? Have you looked before?"

She followed me, picking her way over the stones, down the gravelly bank to the water. "I guess people have looked. It was over fifty years ago, so I don't imagine anything's left, but let's see!"

Keeping our sneakers on, we waded into the stream. I wasn't too worried about snakes this time; they liked quieter, darker water. I put my fingers into the stream and felt around on the bottom. Nice, clean gravel, nice round stones. Nothing gucky or slimy. Lena was nearby, bent over and searching, too. Maybe I was getting braver.

We spent some time like that, wandering downstream and then circling back again. Suddenly, I felt something. I brought it up.

"Oh, it's just a piece of old wood." I was so disappointed. I wanted a souvenir of my summer with Lena May to take back home with me.

"Maybe it's not wood." Lena came and stood by my shoulder. "Look. See how it's shaped—it goes in here, just like a piano key." She wiped it on her shirt and held it up to the light. It was a dull golden brown, like an old elephant's tooth. Now I could see the squared off shape at the end, though the water had blunted it a bit.

"Maybe it is! Maybe it's one of Homer's keys!" I shouted. "Can I keep it Lena?"

"Sure, you found it. Take it home with you." We scrambled out of the water, up the bank, and out to the road. I was so happy that for a moment I didn't even think about going back to my real home, and how soon that would be.

When we reached the cabin, Ma was sitting in the kitchen sipping root beer. "Come on in, girls, and have some. Your gran gave me a whole jar of this, Lena May."

Lena May put her elbows on the table. "What did you say to her?"

"That's between Gran and me, Lena, but she's going to go to a clinic over in Sweetwater where they'll help her with her sleepwalking. She knows she's got to get some help."

Lena nodded, frowned for a minute, and stared at the table. Ma reached out and softly rubbed the back of her hand.

"It'll be all right, Lena, you'll see. Your gran's a strong woman."

Lena looked up then and smiled at Ma. "Thanks, thanks, Mrs. Williams. Katy here helped me a lot."

"I know," Ma said, and looked at me. "Katy cares about people. It's one of the things that makes her special."

I ducked my head, embarrassed. It was nice to hear those good words, but they made my neck prickle. Maybe helping people was more important than adventures and bravery. I remembered the advertisement I'd thought of for the perfect job: "no adventure wanted; no bravery needed." I was beginning to think I'd found the in-between way.

We drank that dark, fizzy soda, and it slipped down my throat so easy that I almost cried. I was going to have to leave in seven days. No more root beer. No more Lena May.

Sadly I said, "We're going to have to go home in a week, Lena May. No more piano stream. No more mummy fingers and mummy eyeballs." I began to giggle.

"Mummy eyeballs? What're they, girls?" Ma grinned at us.

"Oh, just a little treat I dreamed up for Katy here." Then Lena sighed. "I surely am going to miss the both of you. Life just won't seem as exciting without you."

"Really?" I asked. I'd made *her* life exciting? That was a new thought.

"Sure. We had some fine adventures this summer, Katy. Come back next summer and we'll have some more." Then she jumped up and almost ran for the screen door. I remembered how she didn't like endings; just like I didn't.

On the top step Lena turned. "I'll tell you the best thing I see this year if you'll tell me the best thing you see."

I grinned at her. "Maybe Penny Roberts will kiss

for three minutes and seventeen seconds. Or one minute and seventeen seconds!"

"Or no minutes!" Laughing, she jumped down the steps, and ran along the driveway. She still was the jumpingest person I ever knew.

Chapter 18

There was something I had to do before we left. I knew it the moment I woke up. I looked through the window at the pink sky. The sun wasn't up yet. The wind shushed in the pines outside. If I poked my head out the window, the air would be sweet and cool, like rain coming. I knew that four crows would be waiting in the pine at the edge of the meadow.

When we first came to the cottage, I had looked

through the kitchen window with Ma, over the meadow. I wondered what it would be like to step out of the shadows into the hot light of the sun. And it seemed to me that all summer long I had been trying to do that—to stop being scared, to feed strawberries to a pig, to not run home before the funeral ended. But there was one thing I hadn't done yet—something I was afraid to do.

I got out of bed and pulled the quilt up over the pillow. I chose the safe quilt, the cozy quilt. I let Ma sleep under the quilt with the patches that maybe saw a funeral. Maybe ten funerals. Running downstairs—Ma was still asleep—I went out to the meadow. I saw one of the kittens standing in the shade of a Queen Anne's lace. It was watching a dragonfly, and the cat's tail swished slowly back and forth, back and forth. Suddenly, it leaped, but the dragonfly jumped into the air and flew away. I was glad.

I picked a bunch of flowers: first the feathery Queen Anne's lace; then some crown vetch—which always comes up in a long trail like a fish line lost in a pond—and some yellow mustard flowers. I thought of Mrs. Carter living here all those years with her cats and her tomatoes. Maybe she'd picked flowers in the morning in this very same meadow. Now here I was, Katy, fifty years later, picking the great-great-grandchildren of those flowers. I liked that.

I wrapped a twist of grass around my collection to keep it together and set off down the road. I would be quick. I'd be back before Ma even opened her eyes. She was not a morning person; I was.

The dawn felt like cool water. I passed the road that turned off to Lena May's house. I would not go there this morning. She needed her sleep; Gran needed hers. Besides, they would come to say good-bye when we left.

Down the road, past the horse watering trough that grew flowers. Past Mr. Lawton's store. The rising sun shone in the windows so that I couldn't see the orange Frisbees, deer lure, and scratchy mittens. Now I just saw the red ball of the sun in the window panes. Past the schoolhouse I went to the iron fence surrounding the cemetery. I paused and took in a deep breath. I sniffed the flowers.

Be brave, I told myself; *someone needs to remember them.* Ma always talked about memory and how important it was; how it was like a giant thread looping people together over distance and time. I wasn't sure I understood that, but I knew she thought it was important to remember old people and what their lives were like.

I stepped through the gate and a crow rose, cawing, from an oak tree. I jumped and broke out in a sweat. *It's only a cemetery, Katy. Only bones under the earth.* I made myself walk forward past the tall slate stones, past the shiny new granite ones with the letters carved in their faces. I walked to the stone with Helena Long's name on it and all the small stones set nearby with the initials, M, D, D, and I. They stood for Mary, David, Daniel, and Isabel.

They were so little when they died, Ma told me. Maybe they never even got to know what a flower smelled like. I wondered if their momma laid them on their backs on a blanket some days in the field so they could watch the sky and the clouds. Did they see rain coming from the sky and wonder what those cool, silver drops were? Shivering, I knelt by the stones. I unwrapped my flowers and divided them between the four; a Queen Anne's lace and some vetch for Mary; some corn-cockle and yellow mustard for David; and I divided the rest between Daniel and Isabel.

"There," I whispered, "some flowers for you." I tried to think of a prayer I might say for them, but my teeth were beginning to chatter. I looked at the stone beside them again, and where it listed the children's names it said, "Gone Home."

"Gone Home." That didn't sound so scary. That didn't sound like bones and skin and teeth inside the earth. That sounded more like little children opening a door and running through it, laughing. Is that what they did when they died so long ago? Did they go through some kind of door into the next world where God waited for them? And there they learned what rain was, and stars in the sky, and the strange, sharp smell that comes after lightning?

I sighed and patted the earth. The little bones didn't seem scary anymore. Not even sad, really. I would remember their names and say them to my-self sometime. I might even make up some stories about what they would have been like, if they'd ever grown bigger. I would make up some memories for them.

Standing, I said good-bye to the babies, and walked down the lane out onto the road with the red sun rising higher over the hills like a friendly face.

Chapter 19

We stood on the steps of the cabin with Gran and Lena May waiting for us on the grass. Gran held out two dripping bottles of root beer.

"Here, Rachel. Pack them up in your cooler to take home. Then when you drink it, you'll remember us."

"No chance of our ever forgetting, Grace." Ma took the mason jars from Gran and put them in our cooler for the trip home.

Lena held out a green sour ball to me. "Want one, Katy?"

"Sure." I stuck it in my cheek and thought back to the first time I met Lena May. She'd had a sour ball in her left cheek, pink jellies on her feet, and her electric blue shorts on—just like today. Maybe she remembered, too.

Lena began to talk in a hurry. "Will you be taking dance this year? Gran says I can take dance in the fall." She stuck her feet out in a pose and twirled around.

"You'll look great in a tutu," I laughed.

"Not if it's pink!" Lena grimaced. "Pink and red hair don't go together, I know that!"

"You're right," Ma said, going up to Lena and putting her arm around her. "How about a white tutu? They come in different colors, you know."

"They do?" Lena leaned against Ma and sighed.

"Yes, and you will look very elegant with your red hair against the white tutu. No one will look like you!"

Lena May smiled, then laughed. "I know no one will *ever* look like me."

"Thank you, Rachel," Gran said, holding on to Ma's hand. "I visited that clinic in town and they're

helping me with the sleepwalking. Yes, I know."
She looked at Lena and me. "It was supposed to be
a big secret, but I know all about it. You two! Following me down the road at night!" She shook her
head. "Brave, that's what you are, just two brave
girls."

I pulled those words around me; "brave," that
was me, not just Lena, but me, too.

The black-and-orange kitten tumbled in front of
us, chasing a cricket, pouncing on it, and then racing
off after it. Sailing into the air, the cricket hid in the
grass, and the kitten paused. She'd lost it.

"Ma?" I asked. "Could we take her home with
us?"

"Lena? Sure, she can come with us!" Ma hugged
Lena's shoulders.

"Not Lena, the kitty, Ma!"

Ma looked at me, then at the animal crouching
in the shadows, waiting for the cricket to move.
She sighed. "All right. But you'll have to get a box
and put holes in it and some shredded up newspaper on the bottom in case she has to go."

Lena and I raced into the kitchen and found a
cardboard box in the closet. It looked so bare now;
all of Ma's cans arranged by color were packed and

in the car. The quilts were drawn up on the empty beds upstairs. The twig chairs were too neat with nobody in them. The table looked bare without Ma's typewriter and papers all over it.

"You'll come back next summer?" Lena said as we tore newspaper into strips and put it in the bottom of the box.

"Oh, yes, we'll be coming back," I said. "I have to see Horatio again, and Alice, and maybe there'll be another funeral, Lena!"

"That's right!" Lena grinned. "We'll have more adventures, you and me."

"Maybe," I said. "Maybe."

"Maybe 'maybe' isn't such a bad word," Lena said, grinning. "But if you'd said maybe that night we would've never gone out and seen Gran and found out about her sleepwalking." She pressed her lips together and shook her head.

I didn't say what she was thinking either. That a car at night could've come too fast around a curve, with Gran wandering around in the road. It didn't bear thinking about. We took the box outside and Lena and I captured the kitten, tucked her into the box, and tied the top down. I loved my cat already, her soft black-and-orange coat and her green eyes.

One ear flopped down on the side a bit, where one of her sisters had bit it in a fight.

"You'll make sure the others find homes?" I asked Lena.

"Of course, every one of them. Alice wants one of the sisters."

I whispered to Lena, "Why don't you ask Alice about that kiss that lasted two minutes and seventeen seconds?"

Lena laughed. "Let it be! That kiss is history! We'll never know, Katy."

Ma took me by the hand and led me to the car. "You can tell it's been a good summer when I have to drag her to the car," she said over her shoulder.

Gran and Lena waved as Ma started the car and turned it around so it faced the road. The cat scrabbled against her box. I saw the hills, blue and soft as a baby's blanket, flare out from behind the brown cabin. I would miss the hills, the cabin, and Lena and Gran. I fingered the piano key in my pocket; it was a piece of the land I was taking home.

Waving, we bumped out onto the road. We drove for a while in silence. My throat was choked up and I didn't feel like talking. After a time Ma said, "Still mad at me for moving?" She gripped the wheel tightly and stared through the windshield.

"Nope, not anymore. I stopped being so angry that day we went wading in the creek, remember?"

Ma nodded and grinned. "You got me all wet!"

I didn't tell her that I'd felt my anger like dark smoke going up into the sky. But I did say, "Besides, I was madder about the book, Ma. But I'm not now." Too much had happened. I had two new friends, Gran and Lena, a new cat I was going to name Sophie, and I was starting dance class this year.

"What about your novel, Ma?" I asked. "Did you ever figure it out?"

Ma took one hand off the steering wheel for a second and waved it in the air. "I didn't finish it, Katy, but I'm halfway through. I think I know now where it's going, what the story is about."

"Does she fall in love again?" I asked quietly.

"Yes." Ma steered the car round a sharp curve. I wasn't sure, but it looked like she wasn't holding the wheel quite so tight this time.

"Does she *stay* in love?"

"Maybe, maybe," sighed Ma.

"Don't tell me maybe," I chanted.

"Phooey!" said Ma. "Life is full of maybes. Get used to 'em, Katy."

And when we finally drove into our drive, the sun was setting, gleaming on the new red shutters. It was a pretty house. I saw Penny Roberts in her yard again, not quite in the shadows. She was with a different boy this time. And her hair was blond with a red streak down it. I looked at my watch.

"Is that the girl, Katy, who kissed for so long?" Ma asked, switching off the key.

"Yes, that's her. She's at it again."

"Research, Katy, she's doing research." Ma laughed and opened the door.

Then I decided; I'd better watch this so I could tell Lena May about it. I stayed in the car for a moment, waiting. I didn't have long. Penny pushed her hands against the guy's chest and stepped back. This time, she was laughing.

ANN TURNER is the author of many novels, picture books, and poetry collections for children. Her novel *A Hunter Comes Home* was an ALA Notable Children's Book in 1980; and her first picture book, *Dakota Dugout*, received the same honor in 1985. Among her other books are *Rosemary's Witch*, a *School Library Journal* Best Book of 1991, *Through Moon and Stars and Night Skies*, a Reading Rainbow Featured Selection, and most recently, *The Christmas House*. Ms. Turner lives in Williamsburg, Massachusetts, with her husband, Richard, and their two children, Benjamin and Charlotte.